SLAUGHTER OF INNOCENTS

A DCI GARRICK THRILLER - BOOK 1

M.G. COLE

TANGLEBOX
BOOKS

THE SLAUGHTER OF INNOCENTS

A DCI Garrick mystery - Book 1

SLAUGHTER
OF INNOCENTS

1

"Hold steady."

The words are a whisper delivered by stale breath, betraying nothing of the assailant's identity, who was crushing down on her from behind. There had been no warning. The patter of rain on her hood had drowned almost everything else out as she hurried across the car park towards the welcoming white and green lights of the supermarket.

She thought she'd escaped, but a sixth sense warned her something was amiss. It was an instinct that had served her well through many arduous moments over the last five months, but as she looked around, there'd been no sign of danger.

She was too tired to run any further.

As she passed a row of large metal containers, a great weight had struck from behind. She fell face-first into pooling rainwater. Pain shot through her knee as it absorbed the impact, and she only just managed to use her hand to protect her face from cracking against the floor. She tried to stand, but was pinned down. Her struggles made the steel grip that crushed her wrist tighten further.

"Sssshh," cautioned the voice.

She inhaled sharply, gathering all her breath to scream. Then a hand clamped across her face, forcibly angling it so that she tasted the puddle. It seeped into her nose and an inch of water muted her scream.

Now came the fear of drowning.

No. She couldn't let that happen. Not here. Not like this. Not in a puddle in some dark urban corner. But try as she might, her assailant kept her pinned. Something tore. It was the smooth sound of nylon slicing open. She became vaguely aware that her back was now slightly cooler than the rest of her.

Pain shot through her scalp as her hair was violently tugged back, yanking her head out of the water. She wanted to scream, but she needed to breathe more.

"Can't have you drowning," whispered the voice close to her ear. "Not yet. Not when there is so much for us to do."

Before she could even whimper, her face was thrust back into the water.

"I don't want you missing out on this."

A white-hot pain suddenly seared her back, forcing her to scream into the puddle, exhausting all her oxygen. The pain was unrelenting.

She finally understood what a mercy it would have been to let her drown.

2

"Morning, Dave!"

The chirpy greeting stopped DCI David Garrick in his tracks. He was standing at a desk, his desk, he assumed, although he couldn't be sure. Aside from an off-white computer screen and keyboard, there were no personal effects, no sign this is where he belonged. He'd been standing there for a moment, mustering his thoughts before he'd been assaulted with jolliness. Now he became aware he still hadn't answered.

"Yes." What a stupid reply. The last thing he wanted to project on his first day back was an aura of incompetence. "I mean, yes. Good morning," thankfully the name came tumbling without him having to think, "Harry. Sorry, it's just," he circled a finger around the office, "I'm not used to the layout. And you're one of the few people I've spoken to in the flesh since Christmas." Except my therapist, he thought. Best not to let the lads in the department know about that one.

"Well then, happy new year. Good to have you back," DC Harry Lord said with a genuine grin. Not that they were friends, but they'd had a couple of drinks since the detective constable had joined them a year before Garrick had left to take time out. "I suppose it's all different here and with what happened to you..." Now it was Harry's turn to fade off, unsure how to continue. Instead, he decided on a curt nod, a smile in place as he remembered the deference he was supposed to show. "Sorry, sir. Just meant it was nice to have you back. I'll fetch you a cuppa if you want?"

"No, it's..." but Harry had hurried away before he could answer. Garrick hoped he wouldn't return with a drink of any kind. He vividly recalled Harry's brews tasted weak at the best of times, and the water in the office always left a white limescale pattern on the surface. Since the doctor had warned him to reduce his caffeine intake, Garrick hadn't touched the stuff. These days a green tea was a heady rock 'n' roll experience for him.

He sat at the desk and ran his hands across the smooth plasticised surface. When he first started on the force, they had real desks, like old school pitted wooden ones that had notches and cigarette burns to give it character. The new furnishings were bleak and easy to wipe clean, more suited to a nursery than Kent's Serious Crimes Department.

Since he was last here, the department's headquarters, just outside of Maidstone, had been shunted into half the space, and the regular plod had taken over the other half after losing their dedicated station. All part of swingeing budget cuts, courtesy of the Home Office. Long gone were the days you could run to your local police station on the corner and report a crime. Now you had to phone for a crime number before...

Phone. There was no phone on his desk. A quick check

revealed his computer wasn't even plugged into the power or the network.

"David, aren't you stopping?" Superintendent Margery Drury peered at him through black-framed glasses he couldn't recall her wearing last time.

"Mmmm?"

"Not taking off your coat? I know it's not exactly baking hot in here. Thermostat's on the blink, but you can strip off." She gave a small half-smile. Drury was a decade older than him, plump, but she wore it with astonishing finesse. Any thinner and she wouldn't look half as attractive, he thought, then immediately kicked himself for such archaic behaviour. And less than five minutes back at the office.

He'd been single for far too long. Which wasn't helped by the fact Drury was a deliberate flirt. Subtle, but intentional. If their sexes had been reversed, then he'd no doubt that she would've been reported multiple times for harassment, however 'innocent'. If anybody broke the rules; then she became aggressive. And God help anybody patronising anybody else – man, woman or in between. Drury would come down on the aggressor like a ton of bricks. She was, by far, the finest boss he'd ever had.

He took off his rain-soaked Barbour and draped it over the back of his chair.

"Nothing seems to be connected. It's as if you weren't expecting me." He forced a grin.

"I'll get IT on it. A word in my office to bring you up to speed."

Garrick looked left, then right, then shrugged. "You better lead the way. I don't know where that is anymore."

"Jeez, Garrick, some detective you are."

Drury's office was a ghost of its former self. Previously, she had the luxury of space. Garrick had seen bigger broom closets. A chill February breeze seeped inside through a small window left ajar on a near-permanent basis, yet it could not shift the lingering scent of fresh paint. The pinboard that would usually be covered in case notes and reminders was bare, save a pair of laminated CPR and fire evacuation instructions. A reminder that environmental waste was frowned upon almost as much as murder these days.

"Welcome back, I suppose," Drury said as she sat in her chair opposite him, the fake-leather creaking in harmony with an involuntary sigh she released.

"Thank you, ma'am."

Drury winced at the formal mode of address and took a sip of coffee from a mug with a faded silhouette of a film noir style detective. Even the smell of the drink was bitter to Garrick's senses.

"I was happy with you taking another couple of months off."

"Then you may have had a case where the victim had died of boredom."

"Give up on your stone collecting?"

Garrick knew he was sitting rigidly upright in the chair. A sign that he was still tense and prickly to the most innocuous comment.

"They're fossils, ma'am. Not stones."

It was the one childhood interest he had carried forward. What kid doesn't like dinosaurs? The moment he'd discovered that they lay on beaches across the United Kingdom, Garrick had been obsessed with examining every rock he could flip on the seashore. As with most things, adulthood stripped away the excitement. The notion that he may unearth a T-Rex was relentlessly thwarted when he only found traces of trees or the odd fossilised mollusc, but it was enough of a curio to keep his interest. The thought of what lay hidden within the protected heart of a stone still thrilled him, even if it bored others. Cutting the surrounding matrix away to reveal the prize within was therapeutic, inducing an almost Zen like state. However, since the incident with his sister Emilie, he hadn't set foot on a beach.

"Still," Drury continued, "with your sister still missing–"

"Dead," he interjected sharply. "Let's not beat around the bush. I know she's dead."

"I thought they hadn't found her body?"

Just her fingers, Garrick thought. Hacked off amongst the barbarically dismembered remains of some other poor unfortunates that they'd found on a farm in Illinois. Including her fiancé. Beyond taking refuge in the snow, the police there still hadn't put together a satisfactory picture of why they were at the ranch, or what had happened. His sister, perhaps two others, and the killer, were still missing.

Garrick had taken time off mid-case the moment he'd been informed. While he wanted to jump on a flight over to the States and see the crime scene himself, he knew he'd just be hampering the investigation. Off-duty transatlantic crime-solving partnerships were the sort of thing that only ever happened in the movies.

The current working theory was that they would find the missing bodies in the surrounding farmland, but with such a ferocious winter and a vast landscape to explore, the investigators had become snow-blind. Nobody was expecting progress soon.

For the last three weeks, information from the Americans had slowed to a dribble, then to nothing. He had never been close to his sister. Their relationship had been tempestuous at best, but for almost the last year she had been reaching out with various olive branches, well, *olive twigs,* was how he thought of her attempts. They hadn't seen each other for four years. Not since their parents' death, which had exploded in a wave of acrimony and blame that had lain dormant for most of their lives.

Still, the loss was more painful than he had expected. In his professional life, he had always compartmentalised his feelings. It was difficult not to see a murder victim as human, robbed of their dreams and ambitions. Yet he had made it this far in his career by viewing them with clinical detachment. Dealing with their family was another matter. It was nigh on impossible not to be drawn into the emotional vortex that formed around a grieving family. He had always dreaded such encounters and marvelled at the skilled family liaison officers who dealt with them directly. That job took a form of courage he didn't possess. The tragic fact was, he empathised more with the villain of the piece. Only by opening himself up emotionally could he walk in their shoes. Drift into their perceptions of how badly the world was treating them. He'd read the textbooks and knew the concept of sociopaths was a very real one, but in his experience, even the most heinous of crimes were committed by the perpetrator's misguided belief they were doing the right thing to address some esoteric perceived crime that their victim had committed.

If people were complicated, then murderers were on a whole other level. And in that case, families trumped them all in the pecking order of tangled recriminations.

All David Garrick could do was focus on his own life. And that started again from now.

Drury leaned across the desk, toying with her mug. "Are you sure that you're feeling up to speed?"

"Mmm?"

"You drifted just now."

Garrick pulled himself together. Living alone, he had fallen into long periods of silent reflection. A far cry from the friendly sarcasm he was known for amongst his team.

"Sorry, ma'am, just tired. I'm in need of a challenge, not more moping around the house. That really takes it out of you." He couldn't even recall the question she had asked him. He absently rubbed his head – then quickly stopped and lowered his hand into this lap.

The headache was another issue.

Drury leaned back in her chair. "As long as you feel you're ready, David." She eyed him thoughtfully.

Garrick couldn't think of anything more to add, so he forced a confident smile. Not one he felt inside, but it seemed to do the trick. Drury's eyebrows raised in a sign of acceptance, and she took another sip of coffee. "It just so happens something's come through. I'll email it to you. No printouts these days. Your DS is heading down there now."

"Ah, I wondered where Wilson was," he said as he searched his pocket for his mobile phone. He'd left it in his Barbour, hanging on the back of his chair.

"It's not Wilson."

"Oh?"

"He's been seconded up to Staffordshire when that case you had before Christmas ran out of steam."

Garrick felt uneasy. Detective Sergeant Eric Wilson was bright, reliable, and almost a friend – not that he had many of them on or off the force. They'd just arrived at a murder scene when Garrick had received the call about his sister.

Wilson had kept in touch over his compassionate leave, updating him when he could, although Garrick had been removed from the case. Since the new year, communication had fizzled out. Garrick felt guilty for not paying attention, but the lad did not know when Garrick was returning and he had to pursue his own career.

"Your new DS is Chibarameze Okon," Drury said without looking up from her own phone. "And don't pull that face."

"I wasn't pulling any face."

She looked at him slantwise from above her phone and seemed satisfied. "My mistake. I forgot that, despite your passion, you're not one of the dinosaurs." Battling prejudice her whole career, Drury was always on the lookout for any signs of it she'd have to eliminate.

"I'm 41!"

"And the youth of today is even younger than they used to be. She's a rocket, but I'll level with you, a bit of a know it all."

"Perfect," said Garrick dryly. It received a smirk from Drury.

"I knew you were the right one to palm her off on."

3

It had been raining from the moment David Garrick had woken up, to the instant he arrived in the largely empty Londel supermarket car park, in Folkestone's Park Farm Retail space. Uniformed officers at the entrance had moved the cones and instructed him where to leave his car. The knot of activity around the bank of brown, blue and green recycling dumpsters in the corner told him where the body was. The entire superstore had been closed, and the cold, incessant rain and slate skies added a depressing layer to the scene.

White clad SOCO officers were already there. A dozen small, numbered cones marked points of interest around the site. Standing several yards away watching them was a slender, petite black woman, wearing a long blue raincoat and scarf tight against the cold. She sheltered under a broad black umbrella that amplified the patter of raindrops.

"DS Okon?"

She turned, her knitted brow vanishing as a smile broke

her high cheekbones. Wide brown eyes sparkled despite the gloom.

"Good morning, sir." Her accent had a private school edge. She extended her free hand. Not to shake, but to offer a covered paper cup. "I took the liberty of picking this up for you."

Garrick automatically took it. "Thanks, but I don't drink coffee."

"It's a matcha green tea."

Garrick popped the lid and sniffed. Then took a sip of the still warm beverage. It was delicious, and a reminder that he hadn't had a brew since leaving the house.

"How did you know...?"

Maybe she didn't hear as she stepped around a puddle, leading Garrick to a white plastic sheet covering the victim positioned just behind the recycling bank.

"We have a female. No ID. I think she's in her early twenties."

She partially pulled away the sheet to reveal the woman lying face down, her head angled to one side so they could see her face. Her hands were splayed either side of her head, with her mouth and nose submerged in two inches of puddle water, which was clouded with blood.

Garrick knelt to get a better look at her. She wore a thick coat and a grubby yellow jumper just underneath. Everything was shabby. Her nails were long and dirty. Black hair tumbled beyond her shoulders and spilled into the puddle, half concealing features that hinted at a Middle Eastern origin.

"SOCO find any ID?"

"*CSI* found nothing." Was there a hint of correction in her tone? Or was Garrick imagining it? The term Scene of

Crime Officers was the one he had used all his career. Now the younger generation, perhaps obsessed by glamorous American television, were trying to inject their own vocabulary into things. He wouldn't be surprised if he started finding reports from young officers marked with LOLs, OMGs, and the occasionally smiley face on witness statements.

You're sounding ancient, he warned himself.

"From her clothes and appearance, my guess would be Turkish, perhaps? She hasn't looked after herself. Her nails had dirt embedded in them and the palms look rough."

"An immigrant maybe?" Garrick saw a twitch of disapproval on Okon's face and dreaded that he would have to pick his words with more care. He didn't have the time or patience for that.

"Not necessarily an illegal immigrant."

"That's not what I was implying," Garrick said, even though that was precisely what he meant. "Cause of death?"

"Not sure. From the looks of it, she was still alive when her assailant did this to her."

Okon pulled back the rest of the sheet. The woman's coat was sliced open with razor sharp cuts on three sides before being parted to expose her back. Her jumper and an underlying black t-shirt slashed with one stroke down the back, and those garments had been peeled away, revealing her naked back.

The skin had been removed.

Muscle and dried gelatinous globs of yellowish fat were framed by the edges of flesh that remained, following the contours of her body. It looked like some sick Damien Hirst sculpture.

Dropping the corner of the sheet, DS Okon covered her

mouth and gagged. Garrick was impressed that she held her ground. He moved for a closer look at the cut.

"It looks smooth. No hack marks that I can see. Like a hunter skinning his catch."

"Why would anybody do this?"

Garrick motioned she should replace the sheet and stood up. He looked around the car park.

"That's the question. Some illegal immigrants come over with tattoos," he tapped his own forearm, "with bank codes for laundered money, that sort of thing. But I doubt anybody would tattoo it on their back."

He stepped away, slowly walking around the recycling bank.

"The killer didn't go to any lengths to hide the body."

Okon followed him, lining herself up to see his point of view. The victim's upper torso was clearly visible from almost anywhere in the carpark.

"He didn't care if she was found or not."

"Or he wanted her to be found."

The superstore's car park was secluded enough from the rest of the retail park. He could just see a McDonald's with a queue of traffic in the drive-through lane. A large dirty white American-style motorhome was parked on the road and behind it, a pet shop delivery van. As he watched, a couple of local reporters climbed from their cars, protecting their SLRs from the rain as they approached the police line. Even on the busiest of nights, Garrick doubted anybody at the restaurant would have seen anything down here. "Check Maccies for any surveillance cameras."

"I already have. They have one in the car park and the others around the drive-through, and two inside. We're getting their recordings."

"And the shop–"

"Closes at ten. The body was found by a member of staff gathering trollies at quarter past seven this morning."

Garrick glanced at his watch; it was a nice black diver's piece from Guess, with a red inner ring. He'd bought it in duty free one holiday a decade ago and loved it ever since. It was twenty-past ten already.

"How long have you been here?"

"About an hour, sir. I've already interviewed him, but if you want to ask him anything…"

Garrick gave her a bemused smile. "I'm sure there is nothing more I can add to your thorough coverage."

Okon straightened with a sense of pride. Garrick had intended to be sarcastic, but it had come out as a genuine compliment. In fact, he was feeling a little redundant. His previous DS had been good, always following correct procedure, but he hadn't actually employed any initiative and done anything without being told. Well, at least Okon hadn't yet gathered any general statements.

She pulled out her notepad, a sensible black leather one filled with perfectly legible writing, not the scrawl he associated with most coppers, which was one step away from a doctor's handwriting.

"I took some general statements from the McDonald's manager and a couple of staff. They often have many foreigners pass through on the way to Dover or waiting for the Channel Tunnel, but they admit some look a little rougher and hungrier."

Garrick silently prompted her to explain.

"Possible illegal immigrants."

"Fancy that," Garrick added sarcastically. Since Brexit, illegal immigration continued pretty much as before. So much for safeguarding the borders. The poor deluded sods were convinced that the UK was some bright centre point of ideal life. He looked up at the sky as fat raindrops struck his eye, forcing him to squint. What he wouldn't give to be lying on the beach in Spain, complaining about how hot it was.

"Although the Londel manager," she indicated the superstore, "said they seldom came this far down the park."

"Hard to microwave a ready meal when you're sleeping rough."

Garrick watched a line of SOCOs in their damp white coveralls as they slowly marched across the car park, looking for any evidence. There were many black tyre marks across the asphalt, and each one was being photographed. Londel must get thousands of people through the door each day, so it was improbable anything would stand out. It would add a mountain of useless data to the case file, but it was all necessary. Just in case.

Just in case. That had become his career mantra. He turned away from the shop and looked beyond the recycling bank at the tall trees lining the perimeter of the retail park.

"How do you think she got here?" he asked thoughtfully.

Okon folded her pad shut and put it back in the inside pocket of her jacket.

"Hard to say at this point, sir. She's too far from the shops, so maybe she was killed elsewhere and dumped here."

"Mmm..." Garrick walked back to the body, circling once more around it until he stood at the edge of the grass verge next to the trees. Through them, he could see a housing estate. About sixty yards away was a paved walkway that residents used to access the shops.

"Those recycling containers, that one there is for old clothes."

"Yes. So?"

"From the way she's dressed, she could well be homeless. What if she came here for fresh clothing?"

"So she was a victim of circumstance. The killer acted on impulse."

"It's a line to consider."

He finished his tea in one long gulp and motioned to throw it in a nearby bin, but stopped himself. This was a crime scene. The bins would all be emptied and examined back in a lab. Instead, he scrunched up the cup and put it in his coat pocket. He took out his mobile phone and had problems unlocking it as rain splattered the screen. Okon came to his rescue with the umbrella.

While he wasn't completely au fait with technology, the tech boom in the nineties had bypassed him completely. He felt pretty adept at using his phone, at least. Accessing Google maps, he zoomed out of their position. Busy A-roads surrounded the retail park, with the M20 to the north. A quarter mile northwest was the Eurotunnel terminal. "This is a risky place for a murder," he said.

"Sorry?"

"Even with the shop closed, there are only a few entry points to the park." He moved around the map to show her. "I count four roads entering, possibly five, but still not many. That restricts vehicle access. Housing estates on three sides," he indicated the map's east, south and west. "And a motorway here." He saw Okon wasn't quite following. In his mind's eye, Garrick was seeing the scope of the investigation already widening to engulf all the resources he had at his disposal. "We will need to go door-to-door. Ask if anybody had seen anything suspicious. Try to gather footage on home security cameras. Any businesses with cameras at the entrance points to the park itself."

He slowly turned, trying to imagine the buildings and roads hidden from view around him.

"The injury to the body must have been pre-planned. It's far too time-consuming to be a spur-of-the-moment decision. Taking a trophy like that is predetermined behaviour."

"Why would the killer want the body to be found?"

Garrick took his time to answer. "Perhaps taking the skin was a message. One the killer wanted to broadcast as soon as possible." His gaze moved back to the journalists, who were aiming their telephoto lenses in his direction.

"A message to whom?"

4

_____

For the rest of the day, David Garrick battled the overwhelming feeling of redundancy. DS Chibarameze Okon had deployed ruthless efficiency in putting the team into action. She and Garrick had stayed until they took the body for post-mortem analysis, then they returned to his beige Land Rover Discovery, and, after the engine turned over on the second attempt, they were finally on their way back to the incident room.

Okon wasted no time in setting up the various work files on HOLMES and organising the investigation. Conversely, Garrick wasted twenty minutes as Harry helped him battle IT so that he could get logged onto the system. For some reason, Garrick's absence had reset all his passwords. It was past lunchtime, but he wasn't feeling hungry. Skipping lunch, he sat reading about the last case he had fleetingly been a part of with his old DS Wilson. He had paid no attention to Wilson's updates while he was on leave, but the recent victim's unkempt nails rang a distant bell.

Opening the case files, he was greeted with photographs

of the corpse. A pretty young woman with subtle Mediter-
ranean features and curly black hair. Despite their best
efforts, they had never identified her and suspected that she
was of Kurdish origin. All signs pointed to her being an
illegal immigrant as no centres or friends had reported her
missing. She'd been stabbed in the stomach and died over a
forty-minute period.

Garrick read on with growing concern. While she was
alive, her attacker had torn open the front of her clothes and
carefully skinned her stomach from below the breasts to the
top of her pubic area. The cut was not as clean or smooth as
today's victim. Several hesitation marks showed that she'd
struggled and received a violent punch across the face to
subdue her. There were no signs of sexual abuse.

Today's case was a carbon copy. Worse, since they had
never made the details public, they were looking at a serial
killer. He couldn't rule out that the skinning was a message.
They were both young women - possibly illegal immigrants.
If it wasn't a message, then they were dealing with a trophy
hunter. Somebody who was collecting skins for some sick
reason.

DS Wilson had found evidence of footprints in the area,
but since they had found the body on the much-trodden
Pilgrim's Trail to Canterbury, it was impossible to tell if any of
them were relevant. As far as could be ascertained, the girl
had walked to her death on a possibly pre-planned
rendezvous with her murderer.

Garrick sat back in his chair and rubbed his eyes. He
should call Wilson and touch base with him. Try to see if
there are any details that might trigger other connections. He
scrolled through his phone, noticing several emails
from *HeartFelt*, a dating website his sister had signed him up

to. He'd been on one date, but nothing had come of it. But now somebody had tapped his profile, a hint that she was interested. God knows he could do with some friendly company, but there was a sense of fear that his creaking social skills would let him down.

He had an email from John Howard, a bookseller with a quaint shop in the village of Wye. He had known John since he had moved to Kent. A good decade older, he'd always proved to be an intellectual sounding board for past cases, and the only confidant Garrick had. John's shop, *The Pilgrim's Tale*, was a welcome haven in the picturesque village of Wye. Garrick tried to shun the bigger stores and online retailers, and favoured the smaller independents. In John's case, he specialised in second-hand books and made all his profits via his online store. The email was to say that he'd tracked down a book on fossil restoration that Garrick had been after for some time.

He finally found the last email he'd received from Wilson on January second. His finger hovered over the reply button. He couldn't bring himself to press it. The next email underneath was from his therapist, confirming their appointment for tomorrow. He'd forgotten about that, even though they'd both agreed that a session after his first day back at the job would be beneficial. Seeing the reminder made him depressed. How do you go about telling your therapist that she makes you feel depressed?

He searched the Internet for the address of Napier Barracks, part of an ex-Army base now used to house illegal immigrants. It was only two miles from where today's body had been found. He made a call to Guiding Hands, a church run charity set up that offered assistance to those who made it across. He arranged to meet the organiser, who had excellent links with Napier. Double checking he had pictures of both victims on his phone, he sought DS Okon and informed her about his discovery.

"Serial killer?" Okon said in surprise as Garrick ground the Land Rover's gears to find third.

He caught her reaction. "There's nothing wrong with my driving. The gearbox on this thing needs an overhaul."

Okon flicked the sun visor in front of her. It swayed with the motion of the car and refused to stay in place. Then it fell from its small metal arm and landed in her lap.

"Your whole car needs an overhaul, sir."

"I happen to love this car." Okon tactfully remained silent. "What do you drive?"

"A Nissan Leaf," she said proudly.

"One of those electric toys?" He laughed. "They might be fine in the city, but this is the Garden of England." He gestured to the bleak motorway in front of them. The traffic had been forced into two narrow lanes and reduced to 50 mph, just to keep extra lanes free for the inevitable build-up of lorries when too many tried to make it across the Channel. Every day paperwork hampered them, rule changes, bad weather, strikes and just about anything else the Continent could throw at them. It also throttled local traffic, making it harder to travel anywhere in the county. "There are lots of country lanes and very few charging stations out here."

Okon pouted. "I have never had a problem. So, a serial killer?"

There was a trace of excitement in her voice, one that Garrick was quick to temper.

"I know how that sounds. Career pay dirt if we crack it, but don't get too excited. We don't know that for sure. It could be two different people. Hell, it could be a coincidence. And two killings, technically, don't make a serial killer."

He glanced at his DS and saw his words hadn't dampened her enthusiasm. Garrick sighed and shook his head to downplay the idea, even though inside, he felt the same spark of intrigue. He had never been part of such a case.

"The priority at this moment is to make sure the press doesn't get wind. Shout 'serial killer' at them and you're tossing petrol onto a fire while dancing naked in front of it."

Okon frowned. "I do not get your analogy."

"It'll burn your balls off."

They met Trisha Warren on the corner of North Road and Cromwell Park Place, just opposite the base. She'd been surprised when Garrick had turned in and beeped the horn of his aging Land Rover.

Trisha hurried to the window and spoke with a West Country accent. "Sorry we couldn't meet closer, but there's all double-yellows around the base." She nodded towards her little Red Mini parked outside a house. A silver crucifix bobbed around her neck. "That's as close as I could get. They only ever let me inside on official business, and that takes ages to sort out. I sometimes think they don't like the idea of immigrants having rights."

She climbed inside, taking the rear seat and introduced herself to Okon.

"I started the Guiding Hands charity for the church over a year ago now. It's been quite a success. We put them in touch with legal aid, help with asylum claims, and try to arrange work placements for those who need it. It's not just immigrants, of course. Anybody who needs help is welcome."

Okon nodded approvingly. Using his phone, Garrick showed her pictures of both murdered girls.

"Do you recognize either woman?"

Trisha studied them. "We get so many through, it's hard to remember." She passed the phone back. "We had a detective asking last year."

"That would be DS Wilson."

"He turned up nothing. He came down here, too. The ones housed in Napier Barracks are the lucky ones, despite what you might think. At least they have somewhere warm and dry to sleep."

They drove around the corner and, after some badge waving and confirmation that Garrick had called earlier, they were allowed onto the base. Garrick parked the car and stepped out with a little trepidation. He'd expected to face something resembling a prison block, with scowling, unfriendly faces. Instead, Trisha leapt from the car and greeted the site's general manager with a broad smile and a giggly, "How are the kids?"

After a brief introduction, the manager, a Mr Daniels, had assured them they could wander around and talk to whoever they liked. The single-story brick barracks ran in neat rows, like something out of an old war movie. Indeed, the site had been in constant use since 1794, and had seen the United Kingdom through every war since.

There were currently three-hundred and sixty-two residents in the barracks, all of whom received meals, shelter, and basic bathroom facilities. Originally, they were segregated between men and women and families, but all were now free to mix.

Garrick eyed the security, which all seemed rather low key. Even though they were on Ministry of Defence land, the security at the gate – and the staff – were all private contractors. As they walked, Daniels explained people were free to come and go, emphasising that they were not prisoners. That comment was aimed at Trisha.

"Sorry, forgive me, but Trish and I have our differences."

"More often than not," Trisha said with a cheery grin. "But sometimes even *we* can work together."

Daniels gave a tight smile. "I'll be in my office when you finish." With that, he left.

Garrick's image of a prison was further shattered when he saw groups of young men kicking a ball between them in a spirited 5-aside match that was filled with howls of laughter and insults in a language he didn't understand.

"Kurdish," Trisha said. "But we get people from everywhere." She nodded towards a knot of men and women with darker faces. "From Mali and Mauritania." Another group of men sat talking intensely. A couple sat on chairs, engrossed in their mobile phones. "We have Syria, Iraq – anywhere there is persecution."

The relaxed atmosphere and smiling faces struck Garrick. Some looked across and waved at Trisha.

"The press wants us to be afraid of them because, y'know, they're not like us. They ignore the fact that these people have left everything behind to save their lives. Let's go ask your questions."

She led them over to a smiling man who kissed her on both cheeks. He spoke with a slight accent as he beamed at Okon and Garrick.

"Trisha, the warrior queen! Have you come with good news or...?"

"Nothing on your asylum application yet. But we're working hard on it."

"Of that I have no doubt."

"This is Karam, from Syria. He fled Aleppo when ISIS

moved in, killing everybody. He and his brother smuggled his wife and children out. His brother was caught and executed." Garrick saw the man's smile waver as he desperately tried to keep it in place. "They made it into Europe via Italy. That's when his son fell overboard on the packed boat they were crammed on. He drowned."

Okon gave a sharp inhalation. "I'm sorry to hear that."

Karam nodded and gestured across to a group of women playing some sort of game, while a couple of young children ran laughing as they chased one another.

"I thank God I still have my wife and my daughter. Others here are not so fortunate."

Trisha nodded. "Despite their loss, they *walked* from Italy to Calais using their wits to survive. Then they risked it all again on a boat over the Channel. One of the busiest and most dangerous shipping passages in the world. They were picked up and brought here. That was three months ago."

"We only come for a peaceful life," Karam said, glancing at his daughter once again. "Invisible borders should not deny any child the right to a better life. But because of this," he rubbed his soft brown cheek, "people are afraid."

Garrick felt embarrassed. "People are always afraid of their jobs being taken. Most of them use race as an excuse."

Karam laughed. "Of course, we come to steal your jobs. What is it you do?"

"These people are police officers. They would like to ask you a few questions."

Garrick had expected the man to tense and put up his guard the moment he heard the word 'police'. Instead, he shrugged and nodded.

"Of course. How may I assist?"

"What is it you did in Syria?" Okon asked.

"I was a heart surgeon." Garrick blinked in surprise, prompting Karam to laugh once more. "I know. I can see everybody in Harley Street quivering that I will steal their jobs." Mischievously, he added, "In fact, I have always fancied being a policeman. You better watch your step." He broke into laughter and clapped at his joke.

Garrick was taken by the man's upbeat spirit.

"I'm afraid our being here isn't pleasant news. We need to know if you recognise these women?"

He held up his phone and showed Karam the images. The Syrian shook his head and offered his hand for the phone. "I do not, but if I may?"

Garrick handed him the phone, and Karam walked back to the men he had been with. They spoke rapidly, and he handed the mobile to the men before returning to Garrick. Garrick was uneasy as he watched the men pass his phone from person-to-person.

"They were murdered," Karan said bluntly.

"I can't say at this stage."

"I have been around so much death that you could only imagine. Even before the war, when I was training, I saw terrible things. You become numb to such horror." He circled a finger to take in the camp. "We are all different peoples here, different faiths, different beliefs, but we are all human. We all value life, perhaps more than your people out there." He gestured towards the gate. "That is because we have seen how fragile society and life can be."

Trisha gently squeezed his arm. "Karam has become my wise man. Everybody here are the lucky ones. Others that make it to our shores aren't so fortunate."

"What happens to them?" Okon asked.

"They join the ranks of the homeless. Just another face on

the streets. They don't know where to turn, who to ask for help. And still they are the lucky ones. The young girls are taken by people just as bad as the ones they'd fled."

"You mean sex traffickers?" said Garrick, keeping one eye on his orbiting phone.

"Yes. Imagine walking from Syria or Iraq, over three thousand miles. Several months without food, water, or shelter. Forget disease, or abuse, or paying every penny you have to traffickers who pack you on a dangerously overcrowded boat to cross waters, even in storms. Then they finally make it to our shores. Their goal, after months of hardship. Only to be kidnapped by a Pakistani or Albanian gang and forced into prostitution."

A cold silence gripped them, finally broken by DS Okon.

"Is that what you think happened to our girls?"

Trisha nodded. "It's the most likely result."

A young man with an infectious smile approached them and offered Karam the phone. He spoke in rapid Kurdish, shyly eying Okon.

"He recognises this girl." Karam pointed to the original victim Garrick had found on the Pilgrim's Trail. "Galina, from Iran, he says." The young man continued talking. Karam translated as he handed the phone back to Garrick. "They met in a camp in Calais. She was beautiful and friendly. They had even planned to get the same boat across, but that didn't happen."

"And that was the last time he saw her?"

"The last. Yes."

"How certain is he that this was the same girl?"

After a brief back and forth, in which the young man became increasingly embarrassed, Karam finally answered. "She had a birthmark here." He tapped his left shoulder and one on her backside. The younger man could no longer look at Okon. Karam shook his shoulder in a good-natured manner. "They are young…"

"Nobody is judging you," Okon assured him. A quick translation and the man smiled with relief. He spoke quickly and hurried away.

"It's *Asr*. Time to pray," he added when he saw Garrick frown.

A group of young men knelt towards Mecca and prayed. Garrick noticed a few men doing the same, while others ignored them and continued chatting. Trisha toyed with her crucifix as she watched.

"Not everybody is Muslim." Karam pointed to the women. "There are many Christians. There are a few Zoroastrians. I had never heard of them," he added with a low chuckle. "And some, like me, are lapsed believers."

Leaving the group to their prayers, they thanked Karam and walked back to the car.

"I hope that was of some use," Trisha said.

Garrick was lost in thought for a moment. His head was once again pounding. He hadn't quite expected his first day back to be so intense.

"You said DS Wilson had asked about the girl last year. Why didn't our horny young friend recognise her then?"

"People come and go. He may not have been here then. The birthmarks, obviously they're not on the picture. Is it the same girl?"

Garrick confirmed that the physical description was exactly what he'd read on the police file. For what little use it was, they had a name and nationality. He had a sinking feeling he knew who the 'message' was aimed at, but he said no more until he dropped Trisha at her car. When they were back on the M20, he told Okon about his suspicions.

"The sex trade?" she said. "Makes sense. Perhaps these are girls who got away, or tried to."

"Exactly. Being skinned while alive is a frightening message to send out to others who are thinking about doing a runner." Even though it felt credible, there was still doubt nagging him. "Thing is that Galina was the first. Other than a news item about a body being found, there were no details released."

Okon picked up on this train of thought. "Then it's hardly a message that the other girls would hear. Still, that could explain today's victim."

"What do you mean?"

"If the first killing was a warning, then none of the other girls, or the public, heard it. So, another girl makes a bid for freedom, unaware there will be consequences. She's killed, except this time the killer left the body in a more prominent position where people will find it, rather than out in the hills."

"That is some fine reasoning, Chib."

"Chib?"

"You don't like being called Chib?"

"What is wrong with Chibarameze, sir?"

"Absolutely nothing. But I'm getting old and desperately need to save syllables. So Chib is okay?"

"I'm fine with it, sir." She clearly wasn't.

"We need to open up a line of enquiry in the local sex industry."

"I'll do it."

Garrick felt awkward. "Are you sure you'll be okay doing that?"

"Why?"

"Because you're a young gir... woman," he corrected himself.

"This may startle you, but women have sex, too."

Garrick racked his memory. He wasn't so sure. At least not in his experience. It had been far too long. He promised himself he'd check the message on *Heartfelt* when he got home. One day back, and he already needed a distraction.

5

Afterward dropping Chib back at the station so that she could pick up her car, Garrick retired home, deciding to visit John Howard in his shop tomorrow to pick up the book. He hadn't seen John since just after Christmas and was looking forward to seeing a friendly face.

He showered, then microwaved a chilli con carne ready meal from the freezer and sat in front of the television to watch back-to-back quiz shows on the BBC. Throughout Mastermind and Only Connect, he failed to get more than a handful of questions correct. That irritated him, as in the past he usually performed so well that he'd often thought about applying to be on the shows, but the inevitable stick he would get from his colleagues had put him off. Now he regretted that decision, more so because he was feeling as if he was plummeting down the cliff face of his prime. Chib had proved that today.

He sighed. When his sister died, his focus died too, and he didn't know how to recover from that.

Garrick examined the rock on his dining room table. The spiralling ridges of an ammonite were just visible above the surface, promising more would be revealed inside the rock itself. He had already prepared it with a coating of acetic acid, but as therapeutic as he found the act of removing the excess rock matrix away in order to reveal the prize inside, it was a task he couldn't do while fatigued.

Instead, he headed to bed and scrolled through his emails as the radio news played in the background. His migraine receded when he'd returned home, but now it threatened to come back. He swore it was the dexamethasone his doctor had prescribed, which was giving him the headaches in the first place. Even so, until his MRI scan, he couldn't risk stopping the meds. It was critical that...

No, he refused to think about his possible condition. *Possible*, because, like all good detectives, his consultant needed more evidence to firm up a diagnosis.

His eyelids were heavy as he logged onto the *Heartfelt* website and scrolled through the profiles that had hit him up. A nudge was nothing more than a sign that she like his profile - even with his appalling profile picture. He had considered putting on a younger one, but he couldn't in good conscious lie, especially when a prospective date would see through it the moment they met. He was dismayed to realise he was wearing exactly the same clothes in his profile picture that he'd worn all day.

"I need a new wardrobe," he muttered to himself.

He needed new everything, but had become a creature of habit. The older he got, the more he feared change. Perhaps that's what he should throw at his therapist tomorrow?

With that, he fell into a deep sleep without having time to

turn the light off, reply to his prospective date, or silence the radio.

The next day brought a flurry of activity. Over a breakfast of two boiled eggs, some toast, orange juice, and tea in a mug that was twice the size as usual, he received an email about the initial autopsy report from their Jane Doe. She'd been alive when the skin had stripped from her back, as had Galina. She'd bled out profusely, but had drowned in the puddle long before that.

Trauma to the back of her neck showed she'd been struck from behind and fallen to her knees so hard she had shattered one kneecap, which had prevented her from standing. Bruising on the wrists could have come from restraining her hands, while more bruising on the top of the neck, just below the skull, came from the perpetrator holding her face down in the water. There had been no sign she was sexually abused. Her trainers and baggy jeans were covered in mud, much more than seemed right for a concrete retail park.

Chib was already at the office and had prepared him a green tea as he walked through the door. He took it with a combination of thanks and suspicion. He wasn't sure he wanted a DS who could read his mind. Just as annoyingly, she had asked one of the DCs on the team, a bubbly young Asian girl whose name he couldn't remember, to prepare a file on human trafficking groups in the area. Whatever happened to the old days when he had to chase his DS with some good-natured banter?

"The National Crime Agency has several operations in the county." Chib sat opposite as he sipped his tea. Behind her, the evidence wall had a map of the area, with only two pins showing where the bodies had been found, and pictures of both victims. Somebody had added 'Galina' with a

Sharpie. "We're still waiting for them to get back with details."

Garrick harrumphed. "We'll be waiting all year. If the NCA has surveillance on them, then they will not let a little thing like a couple of murders give them away." It was a harsh conclusion he'd come to after several run-ins with surveillance operations. Their priority was always to their covert undercover operatives, so extracting any information from them was painful and usually came too late.

"There is an organized gang based in Dartford that ships young women to brothels in London. Run by this man." On the computer she called up a surveillance picture of a squat fifty-something bloke, who was smoking as he climbed from a Mercedes. He had the flat face of a professional boxer who had taken a pounding his whole career. "Carl Sidorov."

"Russian?"

"He's lived here since he was twelve. Goes by the name of Sid. Although he's been quiet on that criminal front for the last two years. There is a Serbian group operating near Margate, but it's suspected that they're working with gangs in France to identify potential targets, but we have little on them."

"Work the prostitution angle. They were good-looking girls, but if they were being pimped to high-class johns, then they wouldn't be wearing clothes nicked from a recycling bin." He stared at the girls' photographs, imagining what terrors they had fled from and what hopes they saw ahead of them.

He stopped that train of thought immediately. Don't get attached, he reminded himself. He sighed and focused back on Chib.

"So where do girls like that go for business?"

"The streets?"

"Since the internet, it's not the cash-cow it once was. Lorry drivers. That's where these girls would go. Get uniform to sweep through motorway service station footage."

"We already have the footage from the ChannelPorts Truck stop on the M20. DCs Wilkes and Lord can start looking through that this afternoon as soon as they finish the house-to-house enquires."

Two officers. It spoke volumes of how under-funded the police were. Crime solving was slowly turning from a relentless deductive science to pure luck.

"Check cameras at Maidstone Services. The Moto on the M2. In fact, every petrol station along there. And show their faces to the staff at Manston. We need to see if it was in use any time when our victims were killed."

Manston Airport had been defunct since 2014, but had found a new lease of life as a spill-over parking area for lorries when there were problems at the ports. At times, they could keep thousands of vehicles in holding until they could cross back to the continent. With so many bored and horny drivers, a black market in prostitution thrived. Because the airport wasn't always in use, the work was sporadic, coining the phrase *pop-up sex workers* who gathered there when needed.

From yesterday's bumpy start, Garrick was feeling more alert today as the old tendrils of excitement galvanised him for the case ahead. It also helped that a solid night's sleep had vanquished the headaches. Most detectives felt like this at the start of a case. The multiple avenues of enquiry meant everybody was scrambling in different directions. Evidence had a shelf life before it degraded, vanished, or was destroyed. People's memories faded and were often replaced with incorrect recollections, so statements needed to be taken as soon as possible. It gave the impression that much was being achieved.

But that sense of progress was an illusion. All cases had an ebb and flow. The massive rush chasing leads would soon peter out as the investigation became more targeted, and with it, the pace would slow. If the investigation team hit lucky, momentum would finally coast them towards an arrest. The sad fact was the case, like his Land Rover, would probably cough, splutter, and roll to an unsatisfactory stop. Unsolved, until somebody gave it a push at a later date.

"I'll get on it," said Chib.

Garrick searched for any hints of sarcasm or a sign that she was overwhelmed. It was a lot of material to gather across a huge county, but he found none as she made a set of bullet points in her notepad, in her perfect handwriting. Not wanting to portray himself as a lazy fifth-wheel, he added:

"I'll go down the Truckstop in Ashford. I know the manager there. It's only a few miles from Folkestone, so it's possible they could've been operating out of there."

It had been a while since he had visited this little nook of Kent, well over a year at least, and already it had changed. Since Brexit, the Ashford International Truckstop had expanded considerably. As he pulled off the Orbital Park roundabout on the A2070, he didn't recognise the place at all. The approach road passed a Jaguar/Land Rover car show-room, with gleaming beauties parked outside, every one of them beyond his financial comfort zone. Half a dozen ware-houses now occupied the land, and a new superstore was being built to cater to the swelling middle-class housing estates in the vicinity. The town had the potential to become a sought-after booming financial centre, especially with quick access to the Channel Tunnel and a high-speed train that deposited commuters into London in thirty-five minutes – quicker than some London suburbanites could get into the city themselves. And all of it close to the spectacular Kent Downs. It would have been perfect... if not for the country's crippled economy and general sense of gloom.

It was just after lunchtime when Garrick parked and walked to the manager's office. There were a few lorries parked up, with licence plates from across Europe, but it felt empty. Things only really picked up towards the end of the day, when drivers searched for a safe place to sleep where they wouldn't have to worry about their trailers being broken into. Somewhere they could relax in, with shower facilities and a decent but cheap café. At night, it was a buzzing international community, by day, a ghost town.

"David!" exclaimed the portly manager as he sprang from his chair and embraced Garrick. Over the years they had got to know each other reasonably well, so all formal modes of address had faded into memory. Garrick was pleased about that; he didn't enjoy the stuffy formality of '*sir*' and '*ma'am*' that the force demanded. Having people who treated you as a mate was something much more valuable. "It's been too long! A year? Sit down."

Garrick took the offered seat at the desk. "Eighteen months, maybe. You haven't changed much, Doug."

Douglas Clarke patted his ample stomach appreciatively as he popped a capsule in his Nespresso maker and hit the button to make a coffee.

"A little wider. And you're a little greyer, but all is as it should be."

"I see your empire has grown." Garrick peered out of the venetian blinds as a lorry entered the park with a heavy diesel rumble. It sported the vehicle registration code P for Portugal.

Doug handed the Nespresso to Garrick. "Fell off the back of a lorry," he laughed, then remembered who he was talking to. "Well, not literally."

Garrick took the coffee with one hand and waved the comment aside with a chuckle. The smell from the rich liquid was already turning his stomach, but he didn't wish to offend Doug, who was pleased with his new toy. Doug sat behind his desk and leaned forward.

"So, what brings you here?"

"Well, first of all, how's Cathy and the kids?"

"She's fine. Still at William Harvey. And Elizabeth has gone got herself into Liverpool Uni. Your old neck of the woods, I believe."

"She's left school already?" Garrick was shocked. He'd met Doug's daughter once and recalled her as a little freckle-faced girl with gaps between her teeth.

"Tell me about it."

Garrick motioned to drink the coffee, but stopped short of actually sipping it. He put the cup on the desk and pulled his phone out – after selecting the wrong pocket twice.

"Do you recognise these girls?"

There was a tacit understanding that prostitution wasn't encouraged on site. Prostitution itself wasn't a crime under UK law, only soliciting for it was. The unspoken acknowledgement was that nobody wanted drivers kerb-crawling in their lorries, and the girls would be infinitely safer in a controlled environment.

Doug studied the pictures and chewed his lip thoughtfully.

"I can't say they ring a bell. But they all look the same to me." He laughed and passed the phone back.

Garrick's smile remained in place, even as he remembered Doug's shortfall. He was a nationalist, if not an out-and-out racist. He had fiercely denied that in the past, even though his views were more suited to the nineteen seventies.

From that point, Garrick had little patience for a social chat. He thanked Doug for his time and went to see the staff in the restaurant. Nobody seemed to recognise the girls. Garrick was about to admit defeat when one cook changed his mind.

"Wait a sec. I think she was here." He indicated Jane Doe. "Oi, Peter, isn't this the girl you tried to get off with?"

The older of the two cooks shot daggers at him. Garrick looked at him expectantly.

Peter walked across and looked at the phone again. The picture had been taken in the morgue, so showed a close-up of the girl's face. Garrick had deliberately turned it black and white to hide the pallor of her face. With her eyes closed, she could be asleep.

"Maybe. The one I *helped*," he spat at the younger cook, who walked away chuckling. "Phil's a moron. I didn't try getting off with no one. But she looks a bit like a girl in here the other night."

"Do you remember what day?"

"Two, three nights back. Three, I think. I wasn't supposed to be in today, but Mandy was sick."

"What's your name?"

"Peter Thorpe."

Garrick sat with Peter in a corner of the restaurant as the staff set about cleaning the surrounding tables.

"You're sure that was the night?"

Peter nodded. "That was my last night. I was off yesterday."

The night of her murder. Garrick glanced around for any security cameras. He couldn't see one. He'd leave that for Chib.

"It was pouring down. Freezing. She came in when most drivers had gone back to their trucks to get their heads down. Normally we shouldn't let the girls in." He looked around uncomfortably. "But she looked upset and was soaked to the bone. Shivering, too. I felt bad throwing her out. I've got daughters of my own, and I know these girls have had it tough. I didn't see the harm in letting her sit quiet in the corner and warm up."

The cook folded his hands on the table and glanced around, keen not to be overheard.

"She wanted to buy something warm. She looked half-starved and, I don't know, like she'd had a bit of a shock. Her English wasn't great, but she had a handful of crumpled fivers she kept offering. We're not supposed to serve anybody who isn't a driver, but we had a load of leftovers that would get binned. So I gave her a meal. Didn't take her money."

Garrick nodded, appreciating the man's kind gesture, but he had to cover all the bases, and there was no room for politeness.

"Did she try to thank you in some other way?" Peter looked offended, but there was something plastic about his reaction. Something that didn't quite feel authentic.

"I dunno what you mean."

"Come on. A good-looking girl like that? I'm sure she wasn't afraid of sex for favours."

"Can't a man help out a girl without being branded a perv?"

Garrick held up his hand to calm him. "You're quite right, but I had to ask. Did she tell you her name?"

"I didn't ask. It's not as if I sat down and chatted to her. She ate everything by the time I started loading the dishes. When I looked again, she'd gone."

"Was that the first time you saw her?"

Peter nodded. Garrick took the man's full details and noted down the names of the other four staff who had been on duty that night. After getting their addresses from Doug, he drove to the nearest two who lived in Ashford.

Both women had worked there for longer than Peter. The first lived in the town centre and claimed not to have seen a thing. She coughed and spluttered through the questions, and Garrick remembered she was the one Peter was currently covering for. The second woman, Shelia, was in her fifties. Despite being at home, she had put on makeup and looked quite glamorous. She kept Garrick talking on her doorstep despite the drizzle and wore a disapproving scowl when she recalled the night in question.

"He gave her a heaped plate of chips, egg and ham. Beans, too. We had a load left and it would be a shame to sling it all, but he shouldn't bloody be feeding the tarts who come in. We're not a charity."

"Do a lot of girls come in?"

"Only every now and again, and only when it's really bad outside. But you should see his face when they do. He's always taking a shine to them."

"So this wasn't the first time it happened?"

"Ha! He thinks he's a regular Prince Charming. He's a bloody flirt, so they should be thankful they don't understand half the shit he's spouting."

Garrick held up the girl's picture again. "Think carefully. Had she ever been in before?"

"I can't remember."

"How long has he worked there?"

"Peter?" She looked to the sky for divine inspiration. "Maybe about four years."

"Married? Kids?"

She laughed. "Married alright. That's all he ever talks about, how bloody fed up he is with his missus. You know, they divorced last year. Or are they separated? I don't think they live together no more."

With much to chew on, Garrick visited another cook who lived in Harrietsham and vaguely recalled seeing the girl. He commented that Peter was a sucker at the best of times. He'd seen him undercharge drivers who didn't have the right money on them. He was always helping people, and more than happy to give two fingers to their boss, who they both thought was a dick. Just as Garrick was leaving, he added that he thought Garrick and Shelia had a *thing*. He wasn't sure if that had led to Peter's divorce or if he was on the rebound. Either way, it had soured the atmosphere at work, which used to be filled with lively banter. For the last several months, it had been dire.

"Peter Edward Thorpe," said Garrick as he pinned a picture of the cook on the wall taken from his Facebook page. From what he could see, his posts were mostly about fishing and Crystal Palace Football Club. "Cook at the Truckstop, which is the last place our victim was seen alive."

It was the end of the day, and the ten-strong members of the investigation team had gathered for the briefing.

"We're still waiting for the video footage from there," Harry said. "They're slow, but promised it by the morning."

"Good. We need to run a background check on Thorpe, too."

A young Asian, DC Liu, waved her hand. "Already started."

Garrick struggled to remember her name. It began with a 'P'. She had just started a few months before he'd taken leave and remembered being impressed with her acumen back then.

She continued. "He's been there for just over four years, having been hired before Christmas as maternity cover, which turned permanent. He's divorced. His wife left him and moved to Canterbury with her new man, taking the children with him."

"Was there a childcare case?"

"No. It seems he was fine with her doing that. Other than a couple of speeding offenses over the last twelve years, he has no record."

Garrick nodded as he soaked up the information.

"Where are we on the ANPR list from the Truckstop?"

The Automatic Number Plate Recognition system was a vital tool for cataloguing the trucks entering and leaving the rest stop.

"Came through in the last hour," Liu said.

"Thank you Fi... Fei..."

"Thanks, Fanta," said Chib, glancing knowingly at Garrick.

"Fanta?" Garrick smiled. "That's really your name? Like the drink?"

DC Fanta Liu had obviously heard this all before. "My dad is Chinese and has no imagination. You can call me Chao-Xing if you prefer?"

"Do you prefer Fan, or...?"

"Oh, I really hate Fan, sir."

Garrick nodded. "Noted." He took a breath to continue, but Fanta interrupted.

"Are we now following the line that the victims were sex workers?"

"It's the most likely one at the moment," Garrick replied.

"But neither showed signs of sexual activity when they died."

"Sex isn't always a two-way street, Pepsi."

She pulled a face as guffaws rippled across the room.

"We have one name, Galina from Iran, definitely an immigrant. Still no name or nationality for our Jane Doe, but we now know that she was hanging around the Truckstop the night of her murder and was acting frightened and vulnerable. The only thing currently linking the two girls is the ritualistic removal of skin from their bodies."

He took in the faces of his team. Harry Lord was possibly a couple of years older, but other than that, he was the eldest, something that made him feel like a fossil.

"We'll keep pushing. Keep looking for connections, no matter how weird and wonderful." He tapped Peter's picture. "We have our first person of interest. Is there anything that connects him to the first victim? Was she ever at the Truckstop? What I would like to see is our suspect list growing a little more. If Thorpe was having an affair with his co-worker, then I want details. Was he abusive to his ex-wife? Dig deeper, people, dig deeper."

6

While he had been dreading a session with his therapist, Garrick actually discovered he was entering the building with a spring in his step. The small, unassuming office was on the outskirts of Maidstone, and the pleasant young receptionist hadn't made him wait. Instead, he was led straight to see Dr Amy Harman.

With wavy shoulder-length blonde hair streaked with darker strands and red plastic rimmed glasses, she bucked the idea of what Garrick thought a psychologist should be. He didn't want the sessions, and in fact had found them useless, but HR was paying, and it was a mandatory requirement that he complete the course as he came to terms with his sister's death. Dr Harman had assured him that everything was confidential, and she reported nothing back to HR other than her assessment of whether Garrick was fit for duty.

She wore a smart blue suit jacket, with a white blouse underneath, and a black pencil skirt. She was about the same age as him, but could pass for younger. Even though it was the end of the day, she looked as if she had just walked through the door. She gestured to the comfortable sofa, and Garrick sat. No shrink's chair for him. Dr Harman sat in her single seat at an angle to him, so she could better observe his reactions. Although she had a pad and pen to one side, Garrick couldn't remember her writing anything down.

"How are you today, David?"

"Have we started?" After a career of interrogating hardened criminals, he hated the fact this slip of a woman made him feel so inferior and nervous.

"If you like. If not, then it's just a courtesy."

"Fine, how are you?"

"You're my last client of the day, so that makes me feel happy."

"Then you can speed through this, and we can both go home."

Harman laughed. It was a soft, warm sound that calmed Garrick. "What I meant was, there is no rush. If we tip over the hour, don't worry, your workplace is picking up the bill." She shared a small, conspiratorial smile.

Garrick folded his arms and settled back on the couch. "It has been a busy day, which is a good thing. I thought I'd be shattered, but I'm not. Quite the opposite."

"Did your leave of absence help recharge your batteries?"

"I think being back at work is doing that. It's giving me a focus. Being stuck at home was more like a prison sentence."

"Surely locked up with the one person you get along with."

"No..." he shook his head before he realised the route Dr Harman's questions were taking him. He was annoyed, but forced a smile and wagged a finger at her. "Dr Harman, are you coaxing me into saying incriminating things about *myself*?"

"You really are a policeman. Suspicious of everyone. You're the one leading the conversation. I'm just listening in, like I would a radio station."

"When I'm on my own, my thoughts have time to drift to places I don't want them to. At work, I don't think about my sister. At home, it's difficult not to." He glanced at her and held up his hand to stop a question that he knew was coming. "No, I haven't heard any more news. I've resisted asking the Americans, because if they had something to tell me, they would do. So, what's the point?"

He lapsed into silence, waiting for the doctor's next question. For the first time in a long time, he hadn't thought about his sister all day. Only Harman bringing it up had made him...

Wait, did she? Was she the one that mentioned Emilie or...?

He frowned, and once again her lopsided smile disarmed him.

"You're enjoying the distraction?"

Garrick nodded. "I'm enjoying having a purpose."

"When did you stop feeling that you had a purpose?"

"Emilie had always made me feel like that," he chuckled. "Younger sister, remember. Do you have siblings?" He'd previously seen that she didn't wear a wedding ring and had hated that he'd noticed. *Dinosaur.* He was suspicions about Peter Thorpe's flirting, when he himself was guilty of it.

"Two brothers. But they feared me," said answered with confidence.

"I can see why." He cringed inwardly. Christ, he needed a filter.

Dr Harman possessed the professionalism not to react.

"I've already told you this. She was a pain in the arse. I reckon they would've diagnosed her with ADHD if they knew what it was back then. She was always fighting to be the centre of attention, and when she wasn't, she threw a fit."

"Like your fish."

"Yes, my fish." She had poured a bottle of bleach in his tropical aquarium when he was fourteen, killing his beloved pets. He had punched her in retaliation, which had resulted in him being punished for two months straight. Emilie, as usual, had got away scot-free, and created a division between David and his father that grew with exponential acrimony until the day he died.

"You still feel it's her fault?"

"Everything is her fault," he snapped. "She's probably responsible for getting herself killed!"

He regretted the words instantly and looked to see if Dr Harman had written anything down. Her pen hovered over the paper, but didn't make contact.

"I didn't mean it that way." He folded his arms tightly, knowing how he would judge a suspect if they had said such things. "I meant she was never a victim. She was always the aggressor."

"You did nothing wrong?"

"As soon as I was able, I went to university and got away from that toxic household." And never looked back. "Of course, she left shortly afterwards, and our parents blamed me for that, too." He suddenly laughed. "Wow, you really are trying to dig back into my childhood!"

"You brought all of this up."

"Doctor, with all due respect, this is not helping either of us."

"What would?"

"My work is helping me. It occupied all my time before Emilie's death, so it's only natural when I go back to it, it does the same. That's no mystery or insight into how my mind works. It's a distraction, a focused distraction, and if I'm honest I could do with more of them."

"Have you gone on a date recently?" He looked at her. "You mentioned it in our last session."

"I haven't had a chance."

"Mmmm..."

"But to answer your question, it probably would help. To be honest, I'm more preoccupied about this." He tapped his head. "Which I think is a perfectly natural thing to do."

He had told her about his CAT scan results during their very first meeting. They had discovered a small tumour that was placing a little pressure on his brain. They were sure it was benign. Sure, but not certain. It caused his headaches and his consultant had decided that monitoring it, to see if it grew, would be the best course of action. An MRI was the next step.

"I can only imagine how consuming that is for you."

"Exactly, hardly the subject of a therapy session. I'm fine. My sister isn't affecting my work, quite the contrary. So..." He shrugged. "If you want to go home early, I won't tell."

The February nights were incrementally becoming lighter as the weeks rolled on. It had been dark when Garrick left Dr Harman, who'd made sure they used the entire allocated hour, but at least he'd missed most rush hour traffic. He rumbled over Wye station's level crossing and across the swollen Great Stour River and entered the village. Window-wipers squealed against the glass as he passed the inviting lights of the Tickled Trout pub. He couldn't recall when he'd last had a social drink. A non-work related one, that is. Something so normal that he was pining for it.

Wye was a picturesque village of stone houses, possessing an unhurried vibe even during the busy farmer's market. But there was nothing conventional about the little village that even boasted a Michelin-starred restaurant.

He parked outside the postcard-worthy church, greedily named after two Saints: Saint Gregory and Saint Martin. He pulled his Barbour tighter against the rain as he hurried down the eclectic main Church Street, which boasted several restaurants, an African safari holiday shop, a bakery, and the *Pilgrim's Tale Bookshop*. It was approaching seven o'clock, but the lights burned within. John lived on the premises, so kept unconventional hours, only closing when he was ready to retire to bed.

The bell chimed. A relic of tradition that hung on a metal spiral and vibrated when the opening door caught it. Every space was filled with books. Shelves lined the walls, with every available inch filled with second-hand tomes. They lay at odd angles, back-to-front, and upside-down. Garrick was certain there was no rhyme or reason to the organisation, yet the owner could find the exact volume he was searching for within seconds. Over the years, John had crammed more free-standing bookcases into the central space to create narrow aisles. Illumination came from several table lamps, the bases of each handcrafted in a variety of Gaudi-like shapes, their light diffused through soft lampshades. Combined with the warmth, and an electric air freshener that issued the scent of burning wood – as John had long ago blocked off the fireplace – created a soporific atmosphere.

"David!" John Howard emerged from the recesses of the room, wearing a broad grin. "Happy new year!" Despite the hour, John was still wearing a smart black suit jacket, his favourite blue Ralph Lauren polo shirt, and smart jeans. John couldn't recall seeing him wear anything else.

"It's almost the middle of February." Garrick shook his hand. He had a heck of a grip for a sixty-something man, but that was what he got for a career in the military. Something he had been keen to put behind him.

"It's never too late to bestow such wishes. Come!" he gestured to two old armchairs in the corner. They were torn, grubby, and bore the claw marks of a cat long since departed. A red dented metal cashbox was balanced on a small table that doubled as the unconventional till area. They sat and John pulled over a small table with two mugs, stained brown inside with tide marks from years of careless washing. "Now, clap your tastebuds on this."

He produced a glass jug from the side. The bottom was filled with tea leaves. A small electric kettle on the floor had come to the boil, and John filled the jug, carefully stirring the contents until the water turned a soft amber colour.

"This is a rather expensive Lapsang Souchong that a delighted customer sent me for Christmas."

He placed the bottom of the jug over Garrick's cup and pressed down. The water dispensed from the bottom of the jug, ingeniously filtering the tea leaves. John then filled his own cup and watched eagerly as Garrick sipped his.

"It tastes... woody."

"Oh, you and your powers of descriptive reasoning," John teased.

"I meant in a good way. A bit of pine... and paprika?"

John nodded encouragingly. "Wine connoisseurs think they have it all, but tea is the choice of emperors."

Garrick's eyelids felt heavy, so he was thankful for the

caffeine jolt. "I swear you try to frighten off customers with the atmosphere in here."

John smiled. "Customers only clutter the place."

Garrick eyed a nearby table lamp. Like the others in the shop, the base was a twisted sculpture, possibly artistic, but Garrick couldn't guess what it was supposed to represent. The lampshade didn't help, and if it had anything more than a sixty-watt bulb, then he was no detective, and the thin shade smothered the light. "I'm falling asleep already. Why don't you get some proper lighting?"

"These lamps are unique! Look at them. Each hand-crafted and restored by yours truly."

Garrick sniggered. "You don't expect people to actually buy them, do you?"

John treated him to a withering look. "I don't expect you to recognise art. These are my Mary Lynch collection. And yes, I have a lot of interest in them, thank you very much. Anyway, drink up," he lifted his own cup, "and bring me news of the world outside."

Over Christmas, he had gradually told John about his sister and subsequent compassionate leave. He had listened without interruption, nodding in understanding, and giving the occasional articulation of horror.

Garrick was comfortable telling his old friend anything, but for some reason he sidestepped the issue of his health. Talking to his psychiatrist about it had actually been draining. His own self-diagnosis told him that the tumour was depressing him more than the terrible events surrounding his sister. Instead, he switched the conversation onto his latest case. John was a bastion of integrity, a holdover from his military service. He'd even won a medal for fighting in the Falklands Conflict in the eighties. Garrick wasn't savvy to the full details, but remembered John saying that he'd been a Royal Marine. When he'd shared details of previously puzzling cases, John had often given him the benefit of his military experience with some impressive insights he had overlooked.

"That first body is intriguing," John said thoughtfully. "Since Thomas Becket was canonised, that set Canterbury up as an important religious node. Pilgrims came, but they didn't originally beat the path. After all, 1173 is a drop in the historical ocean. The trail has been here for a long time. Some experts claim the track was an ancient direct pathway all the way from Stonehenge. The Harrow Way, they call it. And it goes back to 600 BC. We are talking a colourful history of highwaymen, thieves, Christians and pagans."

That brought back the image of Trisha anxiously toying with her crucifix. John stood and disappeared into the depth of his store, still talking.

"Pilgrims were often targets for unscrupulous bandits..." He returned with a thin, red-bound book that had seen better days. He handed it to Garrick. "These are more tales of terror about gruesome deaths over the centuries. The whole of the Downs is steeped in ghostly stories."

Garrick flicked through the yellowing pages. The typeface was small and far from ideal for reading in the dim light. The chapter titles told him all he needed to know: *the beheadings of the lost* souls or *midnight bandits*. John sat opposite with a larger black tome of superior antiquity on his lap. He began leafing through.

"Speaking of pagans, they had some interesting views. We've just had Valentine's Day." That had, as usual, passed Garrick by. He'd long ignored the card industry's fight to sell overpriced tat to foolish lovers. "Well, some scholars think that Valentine's Day was, in fact, the eve of a more serious and carnal festival called *Lupercalia*. It sounds quite splendid to me." He ran a finger down the page, picking out the pertinent points. "It took place in Rome and involved the ritual sacrifice of goats. It was followed by a feast in which naked men would prowl the streets, lashing women, who begged for it, believing the lashes would bring fertility. They'd eat, drink, and pull the names of women from a jar to have sex with them all night." He peered over the edge of the book and smirked at Garrick. "Could you imagine that here? Half the residents of Wye would die of heart attacks on the spot." He continued reading. "Ah, this is what rang a bell. In celebration, they would strip skin from the goats. They called it *februa*."

"The day after Valentine's Day? That's the fifteenth. That's when they found the girl."

John closed the book and placed it on his lap. "Really? Now that is fascinating." He looked thoughtful. "You said the other girl was killed in November. I don't recall any similar practices, but I will have a think." He patted the tome. "Of course you are welcome to stay and read."

John was incredibly hospitable, but that stopped short of lending people books. Garrick had once asked him and received a withering reply: *"I am not a library!"* Since then, he knew best not to ask.

"I may well do," he answered thoughtfully, although he hoped that there was no religious aspect to the killings, that always complicated things.

They rounded off another forty minutes idly chatting about how few people now ventured into the *Pilgrim's Tale*, but the online income was starting to beat his best days of bricks and mortar trade. He was becoming something of a detective himself, locating rare and esoteric books for keen collectors.

Eventually, John found the book Garrick had ordered. It was a detailed text on how to carve fossils from the surrounding rock, and a quick thumb-through satisfied him that it was already better than the few YouTube videos he had been using as a reference.

John showed him to the door, casually mentioning some recent trouble they'd had with a group of travellers.

"Bloody gypsies, pitching up wherever they want. They had the Parish Council up in arms before they moved on to Hawkinge. Did you know the origin of gypsies comes from northern India? This lot are Travellers." He made air quotes with his fingers. "Except they don't do much travelling when they settle down for weeks and shit on everyone's lawns."

Thrusting his book under his jacket to protect it from the rain, Garrick hurried to his car, his mind racing. The pagan element was intriguing, but he was sure it was coincidental. While they had identified the first girl as an immigrant, that did not necessarily mean their new Jane Doe was one. Garrick had encountered traveller communities several times during his career. Some were of Irish stock, but others were distinctly of Romani origin. Was it possible the girl came from there?

7

Garrick had planned to look into his Romani theory the very next day, but the morning tsunami of information had placed many plans on hold. It had started with DC Harry Lord bringing in a grease-stained paper bag filled with hot bacon sandwiches that he had bought from a food truck. Handing them out, he declared it was his birthday present to the team – which resulted in a hastily organised round of drinks scheduled for the end of the day.

It tasted like heaven in Garrick's mouth. It had been far too long since he'd eaten from a butty van. In his view, it was the only thing Britain really had that classed as traditional street food.

Then came DC Fanta Liu's announcement that she had found Jane Doe on the footage they'd finally received from the Truckstop. She played it through a TV mounted next to the sparse evidence wall.

The restaurant had one camera inside, positioned to cover the serving area. It didn't capture the entrance, but they watched the girl enter the frame as she headed straight to the counter and started talking to Peter Thorpe. The quality wasn't terrific. Her face was not in focus, but the clothing matched. She pulled something from her pocket and offered it to him. He motioned for her to put it away. Then she turned to presumably sit at a table, unfortunately just out of the range of the camera. Thirty seconds later, Peter cut across the image carrying a tray with food and a drink, and disappeared as he served her. A minute later, he returned behind the counter.

"Just as he said." Chib tapped Fanta on the shoulder. She was controlling the footage from a laptop. "Anything of her coming in?"

Fanta brightened, almost bouncing in her seat with excitement. "Oh, yes. And much better than that. I was up late doing a little video editing."

Garrick smiled to himself. Back in the day, that would have required a team of specialists grinding through VHS tapes for a whole evening. Now DC Liu could do it all on her laptop.

The TV screen switched to a copy of Fanta's laptop desktop as she juggled files. She found the one she wanted and double clicked it. The new footage was taken from an angle opposite the restaurant, at the other end of the floodlit car park. The girl could be seen entering the building. Once again, the image quality wasn't good enough to make out a face, but when she walked through pools of light, the clothing matched. The time code read 22:24.

"Once I had her entering the restaurant, it was easy enough to backtrack her movements. As you can see, the image quality is rubbish."

The camera changed to another angle, this time from the

site's single entrance gate. The girl entered the site on foot, keeping to the side as several lorries passed her, and took up the few remaining vacant parking spots. She didn't turn left for the food area, instead she cut across the car park, looking at something in her hand.

"What's she looking at? A note or a phone?"

There was the subtlest hint of light on her distant face.

"It's a phone," said Garrick. "Did they find one on her?"

Chib scrolled through the forensic report. "No."

They watched as the girl walked along the line of lorries, then stopped at one at the far end, parked to face the main building. She seemed to compare it with her phone, then walked around to the passenger side door. It opened, and she climbed inside, pulled the door closed behind her.

"Then we jump thirty-six minutes and she leaves the truck and heads to the restaurant."

The image jumped and the time code now read 23:04 as she exited the truck and hurried to the restaurant, head bowed against the rain.

"It was another thirty-two minutes before she left and walked out of the park, back the way she came." The image jumped to match Fanta's narration. On the way out, the girl was fixated on her phone.

"How did she get from Ashford to Folkestone? It's a good fifteen miles. Is she calling somebody? A pimp? A friend?"

Fanta shrugged. "We have nothing beyond this. There is a McDonald's in the Orbital Retail Park, opposite the roundabout that accesses the Truckstop. And a Jaguar showroom which will have cameras."

"We need access to them this morning."

"Can anybody make out the lorry's registration?" Garrick asked.

"It left at 6:16 in the morning," Fanta reported with a proud grin. "And the ANPR picked it up. I have the details." She switched the screen, and the video was replaced with an image of the licence plate. "It's Romanian. A haulier for TransServio, a small company based in Bucharest."

"Get in touch with them."

"Oh, sir," Fanta said admonishingly. "*Again?*"

Garrick saw Harry stiffen slightly. He was old school and liked the formality within the force, but Garrick was rapidly enjoying Fanta's cheeky irreverence. It was refreshing, and she was getting more done without the pomposity. Just to emphasise the fact, an image of the driver's passport appeared on the screen. He was bald and overweight, with eyes too small for his face, giving the impression of a snarl.

"The driver is Mircea Secareanu," she fumbled haltingly over the unfamiliar name. "Fifty-seven, Romanian national. Born in Cluj-Napoca," again she was tongue-tied over the pronunciation. "He's been a lorry driver for most of his life. We're waiting on their local police force for any criminal convictions."

Since leaving Europe, communication with forces on the Continent had become slow and erratic. Not impossible, but the smooth transfer of information had been lost, which had a hugely detrimental effect when the clock was ticking.

"And best of all," Fanta continued. "He's still in the UK. I ran the plate and picked him up on the M40 southbound."

Traffic cameras across the country didn't store every licence plate that drove past them, as that would be a step towards a Big Brother state that would have people rioting in the street. But plates could be flagged up and identified when they passed a camera.

"He could be homebound," said Chib.

Garrick nodded. "If he is, then that's great news for us. All we have to do is wait for him to enter Kent, and we can stop him." Working with other forces wasn't too much of an issue, but people could get territorial, and it would save the hassle if they could stop the driver in Kent.

"I'm monitoring it," Fanta assured him.

"That is some outstanding work. Well done, Pepsi."

She shot him an irritated look, but there was a sparkle of pride in her eyes that made Garrick's spirits soar. What a terrific little team they were. At this rate, he wondered if they wouldn't crack the case before the weekend. That, of course, was ignoring the many unanswered questions still fluttering in the breeze...

The door-to-door enquires around the housing estate where the body was found had drawn no new leads. The woman's fingerprints were found on the clothing recycling bank, adding credence to Garrick's idea that she was searching for fresh clothing.

He spent the morning behind his desk as activity swirled around him. Fanta put Mircea's passport, and a still of the girl entering the Truckstop, on the evidence board. She gave constant updates as the TransServio lorry left the M40 and stopped in an industrial estate in Slough. Each update made Garrick feel increasingly tense with anticipation, and with it came a pounding headache that made him feel nauseous. He burped in reflux, his mouth once again tasting of the bacon sandwich. It wasn't so nice the second time around.

He re-read the forensic reports on both victims. There was still nothing connecting them other than the skinning ritual, but that was strong enough on its own. What was Galina's connection to Mircea Secareanu? Other than her being a sex worker, which they had yet to prove, there was nothing.

He had a nagging suspicion that he was missing something obvious. Something right in front of him, but the throbbing headache was clouding his judgement.

He took a break from his screen and headed to the toilet. Not for any biological work, but just to soak in the solitude offered inside the cubicle. He scrolled through emails on his phone, which comprised of more spam each day. He stopped at a reminder from *HeartFelt* that he hadn't responded to his nudge. Impulsively, he accessed the app and tapped on the woman's profile. She was called Wendy, and her profile picture was simply one of her with a hiking jacket, giving an adorable, dimpled smile to camera. Garrick had seen many profiles trying too hard, but found hers sparse and appealing. Hiking, cinema, and good food were all she had down under her interests. The idea behind the site was for users to discover more by actually communicating with one another, rather than analysing pages of information, most of which was usually complete fiction. His finger hesitated above the reply button; long enough for somebody to enter the bathroom, have a pee, wash their hands, and leave.

Finally, he tapped and rapidly typed: *Who doesn't like a good bike? Would love to know more.*

He pressed send the instant he spotted that the autocorrect had swapped *hike* for *bike*. It was a lame response in the first place, but now he looked like a cretin. Before he did any further damage, he put the phone away and returned to his desk. On the way, a thought struck him.

He called up the ANPR records for the Truckstop covering the last twelve months. He searched for the Romanian licence plate. It had been in the Truckstop six times in that period. That last time was in November.

The same period Galina had been murdered.

"Son of a bitch," he murmured under his breath.

"He's on the M25, heading anti-clockwise!" Fanta declared from across the room.

Garrick made a quick calculation. In steady traffic, it would take him about an hour to reach the M26, the short stretch that connected to the M20. With only a couple of exits, it would be the best place to intercept him.

"Notify Highways. Get a Traffic Officer to escort him."

Traffic Officers covered the UK's entire motorway network in a fleet of green and yellow vehicles almost identical to the police, save the words *TRAFFIC OFFICER* on the back. Their principal role was to prevent blockages and remove hazards from the roads. They were often the first on the scene of any accident. Although they had the powers to stop and divert traffic, they could do precious little when it came to upholding the law.

Garrick called up Google maps and scrolled around the area before identifying a suitable site. "Junction four on the M20. There's a good-sized industrial estate in Larkfield. He can park up there and we can bring him in for questioning."

"Chib, Harry, you come with me. Take a car. I want this to look as frightening as possible. If there is anybody else available, another pair of hands to search the lorry would be useful."

There was only one police car available, which Harry Lord and DC Sean Wilkes took, forcing Garrick and Chib to take his Land Rover. Arriving at the industrial estate, they selected a space on the imaginatively named Perimeter Road and waited. At least the rain had stopped.

Fanta texted them updates, confirming that the Traffic Police had intercepted the target on the M26. The officers wouldn't have any need to talk to the driver, so an LED screen on the rear window flashed the words: FOLLOW ME. Even if the Romanian's English wasn't perfect, he'd still get the message.

Seventeen minutes later, the Traffic Land Rover – a model generations ahead of Garrick's own – turned onto Perimeter Road, the lorry following close behind. It was pulling a bright red trailer, the canvas buffeting in the wind.

DC Lord had appropriated a Vauxhall Insignia and switched the blue lights on as the lorry approached. Both officers stepped into the road with their heavy weather coats on and flagged the lorry to stop at the side of the road. As it did, Garrick and Chib joined them.

Lord motioned for the driver to cut the engine and exit the vehicle. For a moment, Garrick thought he would not comply... then the engine stopped. It started to rain again; fat drops pattering on the vehicles.

"Come out," Lord shouted, beckoning to the driver, who they could just make out behind the mosaic of raindrops on the window. Mircea Secareanu didn't seem to want to move, and it was making Garrick feel anxious. Until now he hadn't considered that the man might be armed.

"What do we do?" whispered Chib.

Garrick felt the gaze of his team on him. He stepped forward and reached for the door. To his surprise, it was unlocked and opened easily enough. Inside, a frightened Mircea Secareanu sat with both hands on the wheel.

"Mister Secareanu, Kent Police." Garrick held up his ID card. Mircea gave it a cursory glance. Garrick gestured with his other hand. "Come down please. We'd like to ask you a few questions."

For another breathless moment, Garrick was worried his request would go unheeded. Then Mircea nodded and climbed down, clutching a folder. He was, if not fat, dumpy. At about five-six, Garrick's six-foot frame towered over him.

"Thank you. Do you speak English?"

"A little." Mircea held up his thumb and index finger to make his point.

Garrick gestured to the back of the marked vehicle. "Would you like to sit out of the rain while we talk?"

The driver gave a bewildered nod and followed Garrick to the car. Chib and the officers took the chance to examine the lorry. Only when Garrick opened the back door of the Vauxhall and pointed inside, did Mircea stop in his tracks.

"Am I arrested? I have papers here." He held up the folder.

"No, you are not under arrest it's just drier inside. Out of the rain." Garrick mimed, and thankfully the driver got the message and sat in the back of the car. He offered Garrick the folder, but he didn't take it. With close to seventy pages of documentation needed in the hassle-filled world of import/exports, Garrick didn't have the patience to look through it all.

"When did you arrive in the country?"

Mircea held up his fingers. "Three days. I take the ferry."

"And what are you transporting?"

"Paint." He offered the folder to Garrick again.

"I don't need that at the moment." He glanced up to see DC Wilkes opening the back of the trailer, while Chib and Harry were now inside the cab. Mircea couldn't see any of that from his seat. "Are you going back to Romania now?"

Mircea shook his head. "Lyon, then home."

"That's a long trip." Garrick smiled, which seemed to calm Mircea. "Do you come to the UK often?"

"Yes. It is nice here. I arrive a lot."

"And when were you last here?"

"I cannot, uh, remember."

"You come here a lot, but you can't remember the last time you came?"

Mircea shrugged. "I drive all over."

The man's hands clasped tightly together, but his thumbs tapped together with nervous energy. While he was projecting a relaxed attitude, his jaw muscles were working overtime.

"Do you have any friends over here?"

Mircea laughed. "I am too busy for friends."

"Sir!" Chib beckoned to him from the lorry cab.

"Excuse me for a moment." Garrick shut the car door, effectively trapping the man, as he'd be unable to open it from the inside. He jogged over to Chib.

"Found something?"

She raised an eyebrow and gave a rare smile. "Most definitely."

8

The clock was ticking. They had twenty-four hours to keep Mircea detained. If they didn't charge him within that time then he would be free to go – which would mean that he would be on the next ferry into Europe and, if they later found evidence, it would take a lengthy extradition procedure to bring him back for trial.

The moment Mircea realised he was being arrested, he lapsed into a sullen silence and didn't say a word as they escorted him into the interview room for questioning. He sat bolt upright with his arms folded.

"I want lawyer."

Garrick cursed American television for drumming that notion into every would-be criminal in the world. He assured the Romanian that one was on the way and tried to cajole him to talk while they waited.

Mircea tapped his finger on the table to emphasise each word. "I want lawyer now."

It took an hour to find a solicitor who looked as if he was

fresh out of law school. Yet again, Garrick wondered why everybody was younger than him.

After just a few minutes with his new client, the solicitor then complicated matters when he insisted his client wanted an interpreter. Luckily, DS Okon was ahead of them all on that point, and had found a Romanian student, Alina, at Kent University, who had her name down on several lists when emergency translations were needed. However, it still took close to ninety minutes, as she didn't drive and had to be picked up. And then she had to sign various wavers and release forms before she could participate in the interview.

So it was almost three hours since Mircea had arrived at the station before the interview could begin. With Garrick, the solicitor, Alina, and Mircea in the room, it was already feeling claustrophobic.

What little English Mircea claimed to know dropped to absolute zero when it came to confirming his identity. Now everything was translated through Alina, and Mircea didn't seem in a hurry. Formalities out of the way, Garrick slid a picture of Galina under the driver's nose.

"Do you recognise this woman?"

"You don't have to answer that," the solicitor said automatically. Garrick shot him a look, but bit his lip as Alina translated. Mircea shook his head.

"You're sure?"

"My client has already answered."

"How about her?"

He placed a picture of Jane Doe next to Galina's. Mircea hesitated before shaking his head.

"For the record, he's shaking his head." Garrick tapped on the second picture. "So it would surprise you to discover that we have video footage of her entering your lorry when it was parked in Ashford. And you'd be shocked to learn that she was later found murdered."

Alina nervously stumbled over the translation as she realised just how serious matters were. She slowly leaned back to distance herself from the Romanian. Mircea said nothing, but there was a flicker of a reaction.

Garrick sat back in his chair, leaving the pictures of the dead woman in place, hoping that they may guilt him into speaking.

"Fine. Then let us talk about what we found in the cab of your lorry. Drugs."

"I don't do drugs."

"It's impressive how much your English has improved over the last five seconds. You didn't even need to wait for the translation. Maybe if I go for a crap, you'll be fluent by the time I get back."

Mircea's eyes narrowed, flushing away any pretence of innocent ignorance.

"I never said you took drugs. I said there was evidence of them in your truck." Garrick had to pick his words with care. After all, the accusation was not *strictly* true.

"They're not mine."

"Perhaps they belonged to her?" he tapped the picture of Jane Doe.

Mircea opened his mouth to speak, but thought better of it.

"You know, Mircea, while you were stalling us, asking for your solicitor, and then insisting on having a translator you clearly don't need, my team had time on their hands, so forensics searched your vehicle."

Alina clarified the word *forensics*, while the solicitor acted indignant.

"You can't just search the vehicle without a warrant!"

"I can if I have reasonable grounds to do so. And please, feel free to advise your client, not me." He turned his focus back to the trucker. "So imagine everybody's surprise when they found a space under the passenger seat where there shouldn't be one. And imagine their further surprise when they discovered that space contained an airtight metal storage unit. Something so secure that it forms a vacuum when sealed. Which means sniffer dogs can't detect it when it's closed."

"I don't know about this. There were drugs inside? Other drivers use this cab, too."

Smooth bastard, thought Garrick.

"We found traces of cocaine. You know it had been removed. You were not smuggling drugs out of the country, you smuggled them in."

The solicitor raised his hand. "Whoa, whoa, whoa. You found nothing in there, but are accusing him of smuggling drugs?"

Garrick's temper was fraying when he rounded on the solicitor. "You know it would be very rude of me to tell you to shut up."

Mircea chuckled and folded his arms. This time, he was smiling.

"I don't know about this box. Or your drugs. Or these girls." He glanced at his watch. "So I can go. I have ferry home to take."

"I don't think you'll be catching that ferry home. We have a nice, uncomfortable cell for you tonight. I'm sure it will make a change from your lorry."

Garrick took some satisfaction that his mocking grin infuriated the Romanian.

"He's as guilty as hell," Garrick fumed as he sat back at his desk.

Chib had been outside, watching the whole thing over a webcam mounted in the corner of the room.

"You have an interesting interview technique, sir. Just sit and make them furious. They don't teach that in training."

"Is that sarcasm, Chib?"

"Perish the thought, sir."

"When people are really angry, their common sense barriers and filters fall away. Did you see how he reacted to the second picture? He recognised her for sure. And before we arrested him, he told me he couldn't remember the last time he'd been over, despite the fact his numberplate had been logged in the Truckstop the same time Galina had been murdered."

"The license plate does not necessarily mean he was driving."

"He was. I checked with Customs in Dover," Fanta chimed in from across the room where she was eavesdropping.

Garrick smiled. "And he'd paid his Truckstop fees with the same company card assigned to him. Don't look so shocked, Chib. It's almost like I've done this detective malarky before."

"Sorry, sir." She looked away, embarrassed. "I was playing devil's advocate."

Garrick sighed and slouched in his chair. "No, I'm sorry, Chib. Keep doing it. There's always going to be something we overlook, something stupid. Ask Berkshire if they can send someone down to the warehouse he visited in Slough and trace his moves. And his delivery schedule was in those papers of his. He may have dumped the drugs at one of these stops."

"Or anywhere along the way."

"That's true." Garrick stared thoughtfully at the ceiling tiles. "There were no reports of our girl having drugs in her system. No drugs, no alcohol... no sex." Garrick sat up in his chair. "So if she hadn't had sex, what were they doing in the lorry for half an hour?"

"Oral?" said Fanta, before her cheeks burned red with embarrassment. "I mean..." she faltered into silence.

Chib shook her head. "Forensics would have checked for that. Fanta, playback the surveillance footage from the point she left the restaurant."

"Now you remember my name."

"Your parents must have a wonderful sense of humour."

"No. My father just couldn't speak good English when he moved here and wanted something he could remember," she said haughtily. "You have no idea how a name like that goes down in school."

They gathered around Fanta's workstation as she opened the video and scrubbed through to the required point. Chib tapped the screen.

"She's on her phone. She hardly looks up. What if she is trying to sell the drugs?"

"So, she may be a drugs' mule, not a sex worker?" Fanta mused. "We heard from the McDonald's. They don't have any cameras that cover the roundabout she's walking towards, and there's nothing else around there. The Jaguar dealership is too far back. Their cameras only cover the fleet outside."

"Ha!" Garrick slapped the desk, causing them both to jump. "Right in front of us. I told you it was right in front of us."

"You mean this?" Chib pointed to the walking girl.

"No. Budge over, Pepsi." Fanta moved aside as he gently inserted himself in front of the screen and positioned the video to the moment they were inside the restaurant. "I mean this."

They watched as Peter crossed to deliver the food to the girl, then returned a minute later.

Chib frowned. "I don't know what I'm missing, but I saw nothing."

"Me neither," Fanta added.

Garrick replayed the sequence again. "She takes a seat, then Thorpe brings the food over to her, but he doesn't return for a minute. And he told her where to sit..."

"Just out of range of the cameras..."

"He stated that he was busy, so just served her food, then got on with things. But for a whole minute they were together, just off camera. What were they talking about?"

9

The natural ebb and flow of the investigation was familiar to Garrick. With a suspect in custody, it was now a frantic race to line-up evidence to press charges before the law stated they'd have to release him. In a cut and dry case, this was the stage where the team was tired and exhausted as they pushed to the top of the hill. If everything fell into place, it would be an easy coast down the other side.

The only problem with Garrick's analogy was that it was a blind hill. He couldn't see what the road looked like on the other side. That's where unexpected problems lay in wait.

Some of the team had been working through the night and were in need of rest. Harry Lord's birthday drinks risked being a muted affair, so he reluctantly rescheduled them for the following week.

Garrick was sitting alone in the office, making a deliberate point of being the last of the team to stay, when he received an email from *HeartFelt*. Against all odds, Wendy had replied to his bungled message. She had picked up on the hike/bike mix-up and replied with: *now that's a euphemism I've never heard before!* Followed by three smiley faced emojis with tears streaming from their eyes. She ended with a hint about meeting for a meal.

He wasn't an emoji fan, although they were everywhere these days. Garrick saw them as lazy and so basic that they failed to carry their point across. Combined with his initial reaction, that she must be desperate if she wanted to go for a meal, he had inadvertently built up a negative picture of the woman based on a single message.

"No wonder you're single," he muttered, feeling ashamed for jumping to such conclusions. He puffed out his cheeks and spent several minutes formulating a pithy response. He finally settled on a simple: *Sounds perfect! This weekend?*

Just as he pressed send, a voice behind him made him jump.

"I thought you'd gone, sir."

DS Okon had walked in behind him, pulling on her coat and wrapping a thick purple scarf around her neck.

"I'm about to." He logged off his computer and stared thoughtfully at the screen.

"Are you okay, sir?" She hesitated before continuing. "You always lapse into these long silences."

"Do I?" He never used to. It was slightly concerning to hear. "Just tired, Chib. Getting back into the swing of things after a couple of months off."

He could see that she wanted to talk about his sister. Other than Drury, nobody else had given any sign they knew why he had been on leave, although his story had circulated like wildfire. Had it been John Howard, he may have been down the pub spilling his inner most grievances over what life had thrown at him, but he barely knew Chib and, with being thrown into the gears of a new investigation, there was no time to do so. He needed to rectify that.

"We've been trying to get our man to unlock his phone, but he's refusing."

Jane Doe's mobile was still missing. The hope was that, as she had used her phone to identify Mircea's lorry, the two had been in contact previously. That would mean her number was logged on his phone, and if they had that, they stood a chance at tracking her mobile, especially if there was some battery life left. But without his passcode, the opportunity shrank, and phone manufacturers were notoriously loath to help crack security on their own products.

No matter how technology progressed, solving cases came back down to basic human grunt work, while technology continued to hamper investigations in fresh and annoying ways.

"You can walk me to my car," he said, standing and slipping his coat on. He checked he had his phone, then led the way. "Where were you before coming here?"

"South Croydon. It was a good place to cut my teeth."

"At the, Met. Shouldn't you be calling me Guv, instead of all this 'sir' business?"

"If you like, Guv," she said with a sly smile as she held a door open for him. "But you seem more like a sir to me."

Garrick chuckled. "That's a first. It's better than being called an arse, I suppose."

"That was everybody's name of choice for my last DCI."

"I think that's traditional. You from London then?"

Chib nodded. "Lewisham. And you?"

"The mean streets of Kirby. Liverpool."

"You lost your accent."

"Oh, it's there when I'm knackered. Or pissed off."

"I'll make a note of that."

They stepped out into the cold air. The rain had now turned to sleet, which stung his cheeks as it landed. The sudden temperature drop sent a shiver down Garrick's back.

"Any plans for the weekend? If we have time to have one," he added. He might as well lay the foundations that they might all be working on the case. It was Thursday already.

"It's my fiancé's birthday. So I suppose I better do something for that." She caught his glance at her ringless fingers and held them up. "I don't like to advertise my status. It's rather a personal choice, after all."

Garrick didn't know if that was supposed to be a casual statement or a subtle dig. Either way, he admired her unconventionality. They reached her car first. The small white Nissan Leaf unlocked as they approached.

"This is me."

"Ah, your toy car."

"That's right. Although you could also say it's the future. It depends on your point of view." She held up her phone, and Garrick realised she had unlocked it with an app. "I used Wi-Fi to turn the heating on a few minutes ago, so should be toasty warm on the drive home." She glanced at his Land Rover, the only vehicle in the lot that the sleet was sticking to. "Good luck."

With that, she sat in her car and was silently driving off seconds later. Garrick walked to his Land Rover and thumbed the key fob. The locks didn't click open. He reached for the handle to discover it was already open. He must have had forgotten to lock it when they returned. The engine started on the third cough and the wipers squealed across the glass, leaving streaks that worsened visibility. He shivered and cranked up the heat. The feeble air conditioning was no better than an asthmatic breathing on him.

He really needed a new car. Maybe if they quickly concluded this case, he should invest in one as a reward? Then again, he really didn't like change.

That night was a restless one, punctuated by vivid dreams of faceless people. He'd never suffered nightmares before and was convinced they were side effects from the steroids he was taking. At 3:30, the ringing landline woke him. The caller hung up the moment the answer phone picked it up. Dialling 1471 revealed that the last caller's number was unavailable. He put it down to another bothersome PPI call. Only when he finally woke in the morning from a terrible night's sleep did he consider calls from the States never had their numbers logged. Could it have been about his sister? The Flora Police Department in Illinois usually reached out during more sociable transatlantic hours. However, his bad dream had given him an idea.

Entering the office, he told DC Fanta Liu to follow him to the evidence locker. He signed out Mircea's mobile phone, and they headed to the holding cell.

An officer was just waking Mircea with a small breakfast tray when they arrived.

"Morning, Mircea. Sleep well?"

The Romanian scowled at him from under his bushy eyebrows. "I only speak when lawyer is here."

"I only have one question. Are you sure you don't recognise this girl?" He held up the colour printout of their Jane Doe.

Mircea looked up – and at the same time Garrick dropped the paper, revealing Mircea's phone behind it with the front camera pointed straight at him. It took a second for the phone's facial recognition to scan the trucker's face and unlock. He quickly handed the mobile to Fanta as Mircea leapt to his feet and angrily charged forward in a tirade of Romanian swearing.

Garrick didn't flinch as the duty officer dropped the tray and inserted himself between the men. "Easy now!"

Garrick opened his arms. "If you want to hit me, be my guest." He was disappointed when Mircea stopped and spat on the floor instead. An assault charge would have been ideal to keep him locked up a little while longer.

Fanta handed the phone back to Garrick. "As it was unlocked, I could go into the settings and disabled the pass-code." She tapped the screen, and it went straight into the phone.

Garrick smiled, inviting another outburst from the Romanian. "That is so kind of you for assisting us in our enquires. I will make sure your solicitor knows that you cooperated."

They hurried back to the office, and DC Liu set about backing-up the contents of the phone. She dragged up the contents of his call list. Four different numbers had been called the night of the girl's murder. Two in Romania, and the other two to UK mobiles.

"What's happened?" Chib asked as she entered, shaking snow off her coat.

"I think our Fanta may have cracked the case open."

Liu beamed from the praise, then whispered to Garrick. "Was that actually legal?"

"Let's not worry about the technicalities," he whispered back with a smile.

DS Okon took the call log and set about matching the numbers with the phone network. By the time the rest of the team arrived, there was a buzz of excitement percolating the air as Chib revealed her results. Four phone numbers had been written on a whiteboard.

"This number has been confirmed as his home number in Bucharest. Presumably to his wife. The other to his haulage company." She struck through both numbers with a red pen, then pointed to the first UK mobile number. "O2 have confirmed this belongs to Peter Edward Thorpe, the cook at the Truckstop."

A ripple of excitement moved through the room. Garrick could feel the fingers of the law slowly reaching for the scruff of the villain's neck. Whoever that turned out to be.

"He called him from the Ferry prior to arrival, then at 18:13 the night our girl died. Interestingly, we tracked through the footage and Mircea never went inside the restaurant that night. He only did so the following morning for breakfast when Peter Thorpe *wasn't* on duty."

"He was actively avoiding being seen with him," Garrick said.

"After the victim left the restaurant, there were a bunch of calls between Thorpe and Mircea. Five in all. But she didn't answer them."

"There was no communication since, so whatever their business was, it concluded then. Now this number," she underlined the remaining one. "Is a Vodaphone pay-as-you-go service. The user is unregistered, so the working assumption is that it belongs to our girl. He called it forty minutes before she arrived. Just one call."

Garrick joined Chib at the evidence wall as she moved to the map of the area. "We know she was using her phone after seeing Mircea. The network picked up her number on these mobile phone masts here and here." Chib placed pins on the map around the Truckstop. "So she would be somewhere at the centre of this circle. Then we have a gap in our history before her phone connects to masts in Folkestone, a mile from where she was found. This was four hours later and fourteen miles from the Truckstop."

"Her phone was connecting to masts here, here, around the time of her death." Chib circled three transmitter masts around Folkestone, two close to the retail park. "She tried to make a call. Then nothing. And without her phone's IMEI, we can't track her movements between these locations." She shaded in an area between the masts. "Judging from the information we have at hand, it places her phone in this area, which incorporates this space between where the M20 becomes the A20 and the A259. It's all fields. And this area." She indicated a section north of the motorway, which extended up to the point the Eurotunnel tracks entered the hillside and didn't emerge until France. "An area known as Castle Hill, and it extends to Crete Road here."

Garrick took over. "It's a large area to cover, but we have little choice. Her phone is there somewhere. Harry, I want you to coordinate the search teams."

"Yes, sir."

"I think we have enough circumstantial evidence to link Mircea to the killing, so I have applied to keep him in for the full ninety-six hours the law kindly gives us. However, some of the more bright-eyed and bushy tailed amongst you will have already seen a flaw in our line of enquiry." He tapped Mircea's picture. "Our good Romanian didn't leave his truck at all, from the moment he arrived, to breakfast. That is confirmed on video. So that rules him out as our killer, unless he is some Eastern European Houdini. But it does point directly to the one person who had direct contact with our girl and lied about it." He tapped Peter Thorpe's picture. "The problem is that all our evidence is circumstantial. We need that phone. We need to find out what Mircea, Thorpe, and our girl were involved in, and we need to place Thorpe at the murder scene. And we need to do it in the remaining seventy-eight hours before our star witness buggers off home."

"It's not a 'no', David. It's just impossible."

It surprised Garrick how quickly Superintendent Margery Drury could march up the stairs to the fourth floor. She was older and he thought not as fit as him, but he was already out of breath and his knees were complaining. He had to get back into shape, he thought. The last few months had taken a physical and mental toll on him.

"The more people we have looking, the sooner this will be over."

"It's not an expense issue. Not necessarily," she added quickly. "We simply don't have the people-power and I'm on my way to fight a bunch of idiots who want to cut our department back further." Her grip tightened on the laptop she was carrying, pressing it with both arms protectively against her bosom.

Garrick had lived through penny-pinching his whole career. Detective work wasn't just about putting the pieces of a shattered life together, it was about allocating resources. Not exactly the glamorous or brooding drama that excited audiences craved on their televisions. He doubted that there had ever been a crime show starring a police accountant, but the battle for choosing resources was one that had to be picked with care – especially now that they had reached a critical juncture in the case.

"With all due respect, ma'am–"

"Never start a sentence to me with that. We both know it's shorthand that you think I am full of shit."

"I was going to say you are fighting for a future budget when I need the resources today. Now. In the next hour."

He was huffing when they reached the fourth floor, and he motioned to push the door open for her. Drury's hand shot out and opened it first. She hadn't risen to her position by putting up with quaint tradition. She tilted her head.

"You stagger through first. With any luck, by the time we reach the boardroom you may have had a coronary."

He stepped through, gulping for breath. Drury marched primly down the corridor. Up here, the building had the smell and atmosphere of Garrick's childhood infant school. Or maybe that's because he felt like he was a chastised child asking for more.

"With a hundred people, we can properly search the area for the phone. By the time they arrive, Chib is confident we will have halved the search grid. Then a surveillance team to follow Thorpe while we wait for the search warrant to get into his house."

"With no evidence..."

"Just reasonable cause at this juncture."

"Which isn't enough to 'reasonably' justify what you're asking for. Have you seen the news?" Garrick shook his head, still panting. He avoided the news at all costs. "Your case made it national. She's still an 'unidentified woman', but you know what the press are like."

"Well, it was just a matter of time..."

"And since this morning they have wised up to the arrest of your Romanian. I wonder how they learned about that?"

"There are no leaks in my team," he replied defensively.

"Maybe if his solicitor thought a bit of press noise would help his client...?"

"Hardly. With people's current attitudes, they'll have judged him guilty already. And you've just told me he isn't guilty."

"Not of murder, at least. Maybe accessory, I don't–"

"You don't know. Exactly." They stopped at the door to the boardroom. Drury's face softened as she looked him up and down, and her voice hushed. "David, listen. I went out to bat for you when you said you were ready to come back. You answer to me, but I have to answer to others, and blindly throwing resources at a case that, frankly, isn't even half-formed, doesn't look good for me."

"No case is half-formed, even when it's cracked. You know that. It's always a race to tie-up loose ends."

"But that's all you have. Loose ends. A suspect in custody who couldn't have killed the girl and a circumstantial suspect. Your evidence is so thin, even that wet-fish of a solicitor the trucker is using, could punch through it."

She placed her hand on the door handle to open it, then paused. She closed her eyes and reluctantly said. "I'll find fifty officers for the search. As for Thorpe, until you bring me something damming, you'll have to follow in his shadow yourself."

10

Peter Thorpe enjoyed his day off work by having a lie-in. His apartment was on the second floor of the newly built luxury Victoria Apartments, opposite the modernistic Curious Brewery and a stone's throw away from Ashford International station.

Garrick sat in his Land Rover, shivering as the snow fell harder. He'd parked on George Street and had a clear view of the apartment complex's entrance. He'd come alone in order to maximise his team's efforts to search for the phone. All the gains they'd made with fifty new bodies were rapidly being undermined by the weather forecast's warning of another Beast from the East blizzard.

Thorpe's car was still in the private car park, a brand new sporty black Audi A1 Vorsprung. A vehicle that was well above Garrick's price point, and one that should be out of reach for a cook in a service station. The apartment was certainly beyond his scope, yet records showed that he'd bought it five months ago. Not bad for a recently divorced man on a salary that barely scraped minimum wage. Of course, these were all circumstantial clues pointing to ill-gotten gains. Garrick just hoped that he hadn't had a lottery windfall, or a recently deceased rich uncle who had paid for it all.

He occasionally had to turn the ignition on so that the window wipers could flick snow away. A task they struggled to do each time. He hated surveillance work, considering it a massive time drain. He preferred to let the junior officers do it. For them it was a novelty to sit and do nothing – and get paid for it. He'd considered deploying DC Wilkes, but had a change of heart the more he thought about it. It was the obvious lie Peter Thorpe had told him that rankled. By not coming up with an excuse to cover his minute conversation, he had exposed a chink in his statement. Garrick knew what would come next. A deflection that he had casually asked her where she was from, then promptly forgot such an innocent trade of civility. That was exactly why Garrick needed some-thing a little more solid before they arrested him.

An hour into the operation and Garrick's teeth were chat-tering. The snow was sticking to the pavement and the road he was parked on, while the gritted main road remained clear for now. He read a text from Chib. The last signals from the girl's phone indicated it hadn't moved for a day before the battery died, and more detailed analysis positioned it on the *north* side of the motorway, somewhere on the steep Castle Hill, a mile from where her body had been found.

Reclining his seat a little, so he could still see the apart-ment entrance as he looked at his phone, he impulsively checked his *HeartFelt* app and felt a thrill to see that Wendy had replied, suggesting a meal Saturday early evening. He replied, admiring the fact she'd suggested an early, safe time to meet – then rapidly deleted the message when he thought that made him sound like a psychopath. The app allowed people to mention their jobs, but Garrick had left it blank, under his sister's advice, because she thought telling people he was a copper would put them off. Scrolling through Wendy's profile again, he noticed she hadn't mentioned her occupation, either. Well, they could surprise each other.

All he needed to do now was find somewhere impressive to meet up. Not having much of a social life, he resorted to Google to find the best places for a Saturday early evening bite on the Kent Downs. He was on his fourth TripAdvisor review when he caught movement from the apartment block.

Peter Thorpe emerged, zipping up his waist-length jacket as the chill air struck him. He quickly walked onto George Street and headed to the junction opposite the Curious Brewery. As he did so, he put on a dark grey trapper's hat that covered his ears. Garrick exited his car and followed from the other side of the road. By the time Thorpe was crossing Victoria Road, he was on his phone and only paying attention to hurrying between traffic.

Garrick followed close behind, confident that the snow would obscure his face if Thorpe glanced around. He walked over Beaver Road Bridge, crossing the rail track as a Eurostar thundered past on its way to London St Pancras. Garrick could hear snatches of anger from Thorpe, but the words were lost in the wind. He showed no signs of concern that he was being followed, probably convinced that he had hoodwinked the detective. Good, the more arrogant he was, the more likely he was to make a mistake.

Over the bridge, the wind whipped the snow in eddies across a busy junction that led to the station entrance to the right, continued out of town ahead, or towards Ashford's main shops to the left. Thorpe stopped at a pedestrian crossing, still on his phone, then crossed straight ahead to the Ashford College entrance on the corner.

He put his phone away as a figure stepped out of the college lobby and walked towards him with angry gesticulations. It was a teenager, his skin scarred with acne. He was likewise putting his own phone away, and now they stood on the corner, openly arguing. That posed a problem for Garrick. He couldn't realistically get close by crossing the road, nor could he simply loiter where he was, as that would look too suspicious.

Garrick took his phone out and set up the camera, which wasn't easy with numb fingers. He had left the house ill-prepared for the weather and was now suffering the consequences. He pretended to write an email while discreetly taking several pictures. Then switched to video and hit record. Putting his phone to his ear, he looked as if he was on a call, while he could only hope that he was pointing the camera in the right direction.

The argument continued. Garrick impulsively crossed the road away from them and towards the train station, just as the pedestrian light turned green. On the other side, he saw the teenager was walking away, then stopped and dragged himself back into the argument. The other side of the street gave Garrick a good vantage point, and he circled around towards a pizza shop a little further up, perfectly poised to snag the student population – just as the teenager again stormed away from the argument, towards the town centre, and away from Garrick. Thorpe hurried after him, still shouting. Garrick darted back across the main road just as the lights changed and traffic inched forward. In his haste, he slipped on the sludge on the road, forcing a bus to hit its brakes. The driver rudely gestured and silently swore at

Garrick. The move had brought Garrick almost full circle at the junction, but at least on the same side of the road as Thorpe.

His targets quickened their pace, passing several large semi-detached houses that had been converted into offices, their front driveways providing parking spaces: a solicitor, a dentist, and an accountant, before finally stepping into the driveway outside a dry cleaner.

The student had stopped at a battered red Honda hatchback and was stabbing a finger accusingly at Thorpe. Then the teenager unlocked the back of the hatchback, revealing a cardboard box with several white packages, the size of sugar bags, bound in clear plastic.

Garrick's heart pounded. It had to be drugs, but if he'd made a mistake and this was some awful cookery exchange, then he knew he may lose the chance to collar his suspect forever. He had to act now.

He ran forward, his hand searching for his police ID he usually kept in his wallet pocket.

"Police! You're under arrest!"

The student moved like greased lightning. His eyes widened, and he snarled at Thorpe.

"You bastard!" With that, he threw himself headlong through the hedge dividing the next property.

Peter Thorpe instantly recognised Garrick. He raised his hands, then some inner demon seized control, and he sprinted out of the car park. Garrick sprang in pursuit as Thorpe ran across Elwick Road, his feet skidding as he tried to avoid a taxi honking its horn as he cut across its path. Luckily, the road was a semi-pedestrianised area limiting speeds to 20mph. Thorpe bounced off the bonnet and continued across the road.

Garrick's arms pumped as he pursued him in what he considered was the most unspectacular chase in police history. Reaching the other side of the street, Thorpe slipped on the fresh snow – and Garrick cannoned into him. Both men slammed bodily into the narrow trunk of a tree, one of many lining the side of the road. Thorpe dropped to the floor, Garrick pinning him down. The snow that had been clinging to the boughs of the tree fell on them both.

"You're nicked, Thorpe!"

"Okay! Okay!" he panted, evidently physically broken by the tiny jaunt across the street. Unlike the movies, Garrick didn't carry handcuffs with him, so keeping Thorpe pinned in the snow with one knee, he had to phone for assistance. By the time a marked car arrived, Garrick couldn't feel his toes, and judged it to be the most awkward arrest of his career. Still, with very little effort, he had got the bastard.

Very few cases had ever been resolved so easily.

11

I t turned out not to be so easy after all.

Unlike his partner in crime, Peter Thorpe was talking from the moment the recording started in the station, only pausing twenty minutes later when his solicitor arrived to warn him not to say anything.

"I think we're beyond that," Garrick said. "Your client is a delightfully chatty chap. It seems he has a lot he wants to get off his chest. Isn't that right, Peter?"

"Those drugs weren't mine. I'm just a middleman."

Garrick guessed Thorpe was unaware that they'd already made the connection between him and Mircea, or that the Romanian had been arrested. The phone records showed that the two men hadn't communicated since that night. For now, his ignorance served Garrick well.

"A well-paid middleman."

"Honest, I haven't been doing this for long. It's addictive, y'know?"

"You're a user?"

Thorpe was offended. "No! Do I look like an idiot? I meant the money. The money is addictive."

Since he was being so open, Garrick ordered a coffee and jam doughnut for the man, and sat back as he crammed it in his mouth and continued his unprompted confession.

"He brought the stuff over and had his little network dropping it off locally. East Kent was my patch. But, like I said, none of this was my idea."

Garrick dripped the pressure on him. "Really? It feels to me like you're top dog. I've seen your car. I've seen your apartment. All very nice. You're a smart man. You can obviously handle an operation of this size."

Thorpe held up his hands in panic. "No, no, no! I swear I'm just a fixer." Garrick smiled inwardly; *keep talking you idiot.* "Last year, this trucker approached me. A Romanian fella. I was going through my divorce and was broke. I suppose he heard me bitching about it all to Shelia." He hesitated. "We were seeing each other for a bit. But when this started up, I had to dump her. I didn't think she could keep her mouth shut." He had the grace to look genuinely upset about that. Then he sipped his coffee and continued, his hands wrapped around the cup for warmth.

"He told me about this network he had across the country that bought cocaine from him. Just a few people, but his bloke in the southeast had gone."

"Gone?"

"I didn't ask. Probably moved somewhere nicer." He shrugged. "It was a small operation; we're not talking Breaking Bad and kneecapping people here. He said he had a method of bringing drugs over that couldn't be detected. Reckon he had the risky bit, and all I had to do was get it out there. Like I said, I was broke and desperate and, even after the first conversation, I could see I could be easily making thirty, forty grand every couple of months. I couldn't earn that in four years! Who could resist that?"

Garrick nodded in understanding. A small gesture that kept Thorpe talking, while it didn't register on the recorded interview as any kind of endorsement.

"I had the chance to sell to a few drivers who wanted a little pick-me-up, but it was hardly Al Capone money. So I started recruiting people who could help me push it out wider. Noel–"

"The student who did the runner?" The local force was combing the streets for him, and Garrick was confident that he'd be arrested before the end of the day.

"Yeah, him. He delivered pizzas to pay for his student loan, and he was plugged into the college network, so he was perfect. When he came onboard, I really started to shift the stuff, y'know?"

"So you built up a network of kids who could sell it for you?"

Thorpe nodded, but kept his gaze on his drink. Garrick let the silence build. Each passing moment made Thorpe increasingly restless.

"Anything else you want to tell me?"

"I think my client has confessed everything," the solicitor interjected.

"Your client appreciates that everything he admits now will help the juries give him leniency when he's sentenced." Garrick kept addressing the solicitor, but his words were designed to prickle Thorpe. "He's clever. He knows trafficking class-A drugs carries weighty sentences. But there are worse crimes..."

The solicitor gave a curt snort and addressed his client.

"Peter, you don't have to say any more. You've said everything you need to, and DCI Garrick is now attempting to get into your head."

"That's an offensive accusation," Garrick snapped back.

"Would you perhaps like a solicitor of your own? I can recommend a few."

The snooty remark inflamed Garrick. Well, if this pompous windbag wanted to raise the stakes...

He placed the picture of Jane Doe on the table, this one taken from the restaurant footage.

"What's her name?"

Peter Thorpe transformed from a resigned slump to being suddenly alert. He looked between Garrick and the picture several times. This time he was in no hurry to answer.

"I don't know. I told you this already."

"Mister Thorpe..." began the lawyer.

Garrick waved him into silence. "We have already spoken about her, haven't we, Peter? I just want you to refresh my memory."

Thorpe's tone changed, his words coming in clipped sentences. "She came into the restaurant. She was hungry. I took pity on her and gave her some leftovers."

"You said she was a prostitute?"

"Maybe, yeah. I don't know," he mumbled.

"Oh. Okay. Only we have footage of her leaving a lorry before coming in and ordering food."

"We get girls coming in and out occasionally." Thorpe shrugged, his eyes fixed on the picture.

"I remember you telling me. I remember you refused her money and gave her something hot. I thought it was quite a generous thing for anybody to do. But what did you talk about? You surely must have asked her name, or where she was from? You couldn't have just given her something to eat and walked away."

"It was a busy night. The end of one, y'know? We had a lot of cleaning up to do. There's no time to sit and chat with anyone. Even the regulars. I gave her the food and got on with stuff. When I looked over again, she'd gone."

"Without saying thank you?"

"She never said a word."

"Okay. That confirms what you told me at the restaurant, and I just wanted to check." He dragged the picture back, but stopped halfway, making sure Thorpe could still see it. "Only, maybe you can help me with this one. The camera inside the restaurant shows you taking the food to her. But you were there for a good minute. And from what I can see, there are no other customers in that corner. Nothing for you to clean up or sort out. It's just a nice minute when you talk to her, away from everybody else. Unless, of course, you are going to tell me you stood in silence and watched a young, frightened girl eat. I mean, could you imagine how creepy *that* sounds?"

Thorpe lifted his gaze to meet the detective's. "Maybe, I forgot. Maybe, I asked a few things, but she didn't tell me anything that I remember."

Garrick nodded and let time stretch a little longer before dropping his bombshell. "So she didn't tell you what she'd been doing with Mircea Secareanu in his truck, for the last forty minutes?"

Thorpe's poker face was exemplary. It was only betrayed by the low huskiness of his reply. "W-who...?"

"Mircea Secareanu." Garrick feigned surprised. "Oh, don't you know? Your Romanian business partner. He's downstairs in a cell. We brought him in yesterday. He said so many interesting things."

"Mr Thorpe," the solicitor wearily chimed in. "Please remember, you are not obliged to say anything."

Garrick wagged a finger at the solicitor. "He's quite right. You're not. Which is fine, because Mircea told us plenty already."

"Like what?"

"You. Him. Her." He pushed the photo back towards Thorpe, then leaned back in his seat and waited.

"I don't know her name." He caught Garrick's eye. "Not her real name. At least I don't think so. I called her Jamal, and she said she'd come over from Iraq. Her English was good, she could have been from anywhere, she looked half-caste to me."

He leaned back in his chair and was visibly shaking; aware of the potential trouble he was in. "Mircea found her in his truck. He introduced us, but I only saw her around the Truckstop. Got chatting every now and again. She wanted to settle down here, but was afraid if she turned herself into the authorities, they'd deport her. Told me she had no family left back home. They'd been killed."

His voice trembled with emotion, but he pulled himself together. "I got daughters of my own. I felt sorry for her. I could see she could do with the cash. She wanted to save and study here. This'll make you laugh. She wanted to study law and help refugees."

This was the part Garrick hated. Until now, she was plain old Jane Doe. Not a person, just a corpse. Now, Thorpe was adding layers of history, of personality. Outlining hopes and dreams that had been snatched from one so young. Dealing with victims' families was always painful for all involved, yet Garrick thought the real tragedy was that nobody would miss Jamal. An innocent victim of fortune. A fighting spirit who had rallied against the odds to shape her own destiny, only to have it savagely taken from her.

Thorpe exhaled a long, pent-up breath.

He picked up the picture and stared closely at it. "This was the last time I saw her."

"Where did she go after you spoke?"

"I gave her two kilos of coke to sell. She already told me she wasn't doing it no more, but Mircea had arranged one last run. She hated doing it, and to be honest, I felt bad for asking her. But she was frightened that Mircea would turn her in if she didn't."

"So when he found her stowed away in his truck, that was the deal? She sells the drugs and you both keep quiet that she's illegally in the country."

"She wasn't happy, but she was earning money she couldn't make any other way."

"That's a nasty position for a young girl to be in. Especially such an attractive one. She must have felt vulnerable."

"I didn't touch her." Thorpe's voice rose sharply. "I never touched her."

"You didn't find her attractive?"

"Of course I did. She was, but that doesn't mean a thing!" he was almost shouting now. "That's what Mircea had threatened her with. When she understood that she might be able to claim asylum here, turning her in was no longer a threat. That's what Mircea was probably doing in his truck. Trying to scare the shit out of her."

"She was also frightened because he abused her."

Thorpe blinked in surprise. "Abused her? He's a bender! Gay." He clarified. "No, he got into her head. When she came to see me, she was a mess. She even threatened to turn herself in and expose us all."

Now it was Garrick's turn not to give anything away. Yet inside the words had ignited a Catherine wheel of motives that led to her death. It was the kernel of a confession he needed.

"That's quite a Sword of Damocles to have hanging over your head." The blank look on Thorpe's face told him all Garrick needed to know about his exposure to the classics. "All the effort you had both put into this operation, and she now thought she had the power to take it all away like that." He snapped his fingers. "I don't know how I would go about changing her mind. She was obviously strong-willed."

Thorpe nodded, now nervously crushing the side of his empty paper cup. He was on guard, and Garrick had to keep him unbalanced if he was to get the confession.

"So she sold a lot of coke, but who to? I mean, your student, I can see the market there. But, and this is probably me being really naïve, I can't see the market in selling to a bunch of poor illegal immigrants."

He thought back to Napier Barracks. The impromptu community that didn't have two pennies to rub together. Addiction of any kind was the last problem they needed.

"She wasn't staying with them, though, was she?"

"Who was she staying with?"

"She'd met a bunch of pikeys who'd taken a shine to her."

"Travellers?"

"Whatever you wanna call them."

"Where are they?"

"Travellin', ain't they? They're knocking around some-where. She told me once that when she gets her degree, that she'd campaign for their rights. I told her it was a waste of time."

"So she sold the drugs to them?"

"I didn't ask. I didn't wanna know. She came back with the money. That's all that mattered. Like I said, she shifted *a lot* of the stuff. That's why we didn't want her to go." He immediately regretted saying the last few words.

"I think it's fair to assume when she left that night, you felt as if she might really carry out her threat and drop you all in it. Is that what you and Mircea were calling each other about? Five calls, I believe."

Once again, Thorpe fell silent and studied Garrick, trying to ascertain just how much he knew.

"Mircea was worried."

"Was that when the decision was taken that she was too much of a risk?"

"I suppose..." Thorpe was suddenly suspicious. "Hold on a second. I didn't kill her."

"Mircea didn't leave his truck all night. After all, he is the kingpin in all of this. He can just drive away into the sunset and never come back. Set up elsewhere. He doesn't really have much to lose if you think about it. Whereas she's your employee, as you've said. If she talks, the first person who is going down isn't Mircea, it's you."

Thorpe slammed both palms on the table and raised his voice. "I didn't kill her!"

"Can anybody vouch where you were between leaving work and eight the following morning?"

"No... but..."

"Peter Edward Thorpe, I am charging you on suspicion of murder."

Thorpe's jaw clamped shut. He slumped back in his chair and glared at Garrick with contempt and hatred. Garrick saw that as a sign of a job well done.

12

At four-thirty, just as it was getting dark and more snow was blanketing the area, Chib's search team found the phone at the Castle Hill viewpoint, close to Folkestone Castle. A site more commonly known by locals as Caesar's Camp, it was barely a few rocks on the earthen mound that now stood guardian over the town. A perfectly isolated place for a clandestine meeting.

The battery was dead, so there was no immediate way to be sure it was Jamal's, but the odds were on their side. Forensics took it to the lab as the team continued searching until the last ray of light disappeared.

Garrick was overjoyed. They were going to have to burn the midnight oil, yet none of the team gave the slightest complaint. There was the unspoken collective feeling of a case rapidly coming together, and that alone was worth any amount of effort. As much as they moaned about conditions and pay, they all had got into the job so they could make their mark on the world and ensure scumbags didn't get away with their crimes.

By eight o'clock, after a brief stop back home to eat, get changed, and warm up, Chib was back at the station in time to receive the information from forensics. The phone was locked, so they faced problems accessing the data on it. As it wasn't one with sophisticated facial recognition, it meant she couldn't even use the dead girl's face to unlock it. Ironically, the older phone was much more secure than the latest models.

However, they had contacted her phone carrier and received a list of calls she had made over the last week. There was just one unfamiliar number. A call made within moments of leaving the Truckstop. It was the last call she had made.

At his desk, Garrick stopped wolfing down the Mexican tostadas the Deliveroo driver had just dropped off. The news had upset his appetite, even though the office was now an abundance of flavoursome smells as the rest of the team tucked into their late dinners.

"What's wrong, sir?" Chib asked, as Garrick stared at the call list.

He ran a finger along a number that had called her twice before she arrived at the Truckstop.

"This is Mircea's number. Setting up their meeting. Then nothing. Nothing from our boy Thorpe, either."

"But we have them in the same location."

"Mircea never left his truck. And he never abused her. He is gay."

"There was no sign of sexual assault," she reminded him. The sex-worker angle had been ditched in light of the drugs.

Garrick pondered on that. "So our motive centres on her reluctance to continue being a drug mule."

"She must have said something really inflammatory for them to want to kill her."

"But Thorpe still gave her the drugs. Mircea didn't leave his lorry until the morning, and there are no obvious communications between the two men."

Chib sat on the edge of the desk and mused. "Maybe Thorpe has a change of heart and goes after her to retrieve the drugs? If she's found with them, then that's a smoking gun. And we found no drugs on her."

"Right. A drugs exchange gone wrong."

"Right."

They both fell silent, staring at the numbers on the screen. Finally, Garrick spoke.

"Feels a bit bloody thin, doesn't it?"

"Like water."

Garrick clicked his way through the computer menus until he found the folder containing the Truckstop surveillance videos. He played the last one, showing Jamal hurriedly walking from the restaurant, across the car park and down towards the Orbital Park roundabout where she was lost from the cameras. Garrick replayed it twice.

"Look at what she's doing."

"On her phone."

"Not making a call. She's typing a message."

"She's using a messenger app. We'll need to access her phone to know which one."

Garrick switched back to the call log and pointed to the third from last number called. "Look at the timestamp. The call was made before she left the restaurant." He replayed the footage, and they compared the time on the recording. "Literally seconds before she left."

DC Fanta Liu hurried in with a beaming smile. "Sir! I

have the IMEI responses from the phone towers!" The *International Mobile Equipment Identity* was a marker unique to every mobile phone.

"Oh, that's good, Pepsi," said Garrick, not quite following her.

"Fanta," she corrected him primly as she sat at her computer and logged on. "And yes, it is wonderful because I can now trace her route."

Curious, Garrick and Chib rolled their seats over to her. Fanta's gaze didn't leave the untouched tostadas.

"My dad always said that it was criminal to waste food," she said with an air of longing.

Garrick suddenly realised that she looked hungry. "Do you want them?"

Her smile returned as she reached for the food and was already scooping mouthfuls with one hand, and she typed with the other. "I haven't eaten all day," she mumbled. She hit a key on the computer. "Behold the wonder of dynamic call tracking."

A map appeared on the screen. White dots flashed from seemingly random locations. She looked pleased.

"What are we looking at?" Garrick asked.

"Now we have her phone's IMEI, we trace every time it connected to a mast, whether or not she was making a call. It sort of checks into the network and says, '*hello, any messages for me?*' Each dot is her phone connecting to a tower."

"But we can't see the messages," Chib clarified.

"Correct. But we can triangulate her position. Look."

A circle appeared with a dot in the centre. The dot slowly moved down Waterbrook Avenue. As it did so, flashes from the phone masts at the leading edge of the circle flashed.

Fanta explained. "The dot is the phone's approximate

position. As she moves forward, it pings the towers ahead so the software is roughly working out where she is."

The dot suddenly stopped at the roundabout opposite the McDonald's. The lights regularly pulsed for almost two minutes.

"She's just standing there, waiting," said Fanta.

Then the dot vanished. Before Garrick could speak, Fanta widened the map, and they saw the circle was hopping up the A2070 towards the M20. It was moving rapidly as it made huge, jerky leaps.

"Assuming she was no Usain Bolt, she's in a vehicle," Fanta said with a mouthful of tortilla. She sped up the animation as the signal moved along the M20 towards Folkestone, taking junction 13 and arcing around – past her eventual murder site – before looping northwards on the A260 and eventually stopping on Crete Road. "Now she's at the top of Castle Hill and walking to the viewpoint."

"Why would she do that?" Chib asked. She saw the timestamp. "It's almost one in the morning. It would be pitch black."

"She's passing the drugs on."

The dot then never moved from that position until the battery died almost twenty-four hours later. Garrick sat back in his chair. Fanta finished the food and put the carton on the side of her desk.

"Thanks for dinner, sir."

Garrick nodded. "So somebody picked her up and drove her there. As good a place as any for a drugs trade. Her last number. Who did she call?"

"123."

Garrick blinked. "The speaking clock?"

Chib bobbed her head thoughtfully. "Easy to mis-dial calling for help with cold hands, in the dark, terrified."

"I would have thought 999 was relatively easy to dial," Garrick said.

"After crossing Europe to get here, I would have thought 112 was more natural." The catch-all European number for emergency services. "Whatever happened after that, she left her phone. To me, that means she was already in danger. The phone had a torch on it. She'd need it to see where she was going. It was the only thing she had on her to call for help."

"It was her lifeline," Garrick said as he widened the map so that it included the retail park where she'd been found. "It's near to the hill, across the motorway, into the car park. Three hundred metres? Downhill, mostly. That gives her two hours tops, hiding, running, as somebody pursues her. Finds her outside Londel and kills her."

Fanta and Chib nodded in agreement.

"But we're forgetting the drugs Thorpe gave her. Did the killer take them?" Garrick sighed. "Obviously, Thorpe could have made the journey. The only issue is that security footage has him leaving the Truckstop roughly the same time her phone stops moving at Castle Hill. It's a twenty-minute drive, maybe a bit quicker if he's hammering it. And why is he going after her now, when it seems she has already planned to sell them on?"

"He still could've made it to the retail park and killed her," Chib pointed out.

Despite himself, Garrick wasn't convinced. "It looks like she was picked up from the Truckstop and was driven to the hill. Possibly to a pre-arranged rendezvous and the deal went wrong. Either with whoever drove her, or the driver simply dropped her off... or she was taken there against her will."

They stared at the map in silence, hoping for inspiration.

Garrick stood, frustrated. "Any of those ideas places *both* our key suspects far from the scene and introduces a third player who we know nothing about. We need to make more connections. I need something that puts Thorpe right on top of our crime scene!"

He was feeling the threads of the case were slipping from his fingers again.

Ah, the ebbs and flows of an investigation.

He hated them.

It was past ten-thirty when members of the team started drifting home. Fanta stayed slavishly at her computer, waiting for more phone data to come in. When it did, her excitement had completely fizzled. She picked up her coat and crossed over to Garrick, who was hunched at his desk, rubbing tired eyes.

"The phone company gave us tracking data for both our suspects' phones."

From her face, Garrick could see it wasn't good news.

She put on her coat. "Mircea's never left his cab. Thorpe took his home and slept with it."

They both had digital alibis. Fanta said goodnight and left the same time as Chib. Alone, and sitting in an office that smelled as if it was the hub of an international kitchen, Garrick concluded coppers were messy bastards. He also mused that the case, which was supposed to bring him back with phoenix-like grace, now had more holes than Swiss cheese.

He should turn it in for the night. His mind was mush, and his eyes dry and sore. He was about to shut the computer down when he had a thought. On impulse, he checked the phone records they had for Mircea. His Romanian phone provider had yet to respond to their request for information, but the O2 network, which handled his roaming service in the UK, had been swift to offer everything they had.

Garrick scrolled through the data, checking dates. Mircea was in the UK at the same time Galina was murdered. Not only that, his IMEI put him at the Truckstop the same night. It also revealed that he didn't leave his cab, either.

Two murders.

It was coincidental, surely. But Garrick didn't trust coincidences.

Perhaps Thorpe was simply caught up in events, as he claimed. Was Mircea the killer?

Garrick logged off his computer and took his coat. As he marched towards the exit. The immediate problem was one of time. They had arrested *both* Thorpe and Mircea on suspicion of murder and had them until Monday. Without solid evidence, they would have to be released.

The thought consumed him all the way home.

13

"A rich and much maligned culture." John Howard reached over and examined three of the scones in the basket before choosing the second one to put on his plate.

The coffee shop on the corner of Church Street was rather quiet for eleven o'clock on a Saturday morning, with just two elderly women chatting in the corner as they shared a teapot, and a tall, thin, stony-faced man in the corner reading a newspaper. Every time he moved his arm, his heavy wax jacket made a crinkling sound that distracted Garrick. He hadn't slept terribly well and had been looking for an escape from the office all morning. A call to John had provided just that. He put the distinct lack of customers down to the new owner's decision to rename café: *Wye Have Coffee?*

"I think most people would be surprised to hear that," Garrick replied, watching John delicately cut the scone in half. "A lot of people dislike them."

"Ah, the old gypsies," John sighed. "Somewhere over the years, the romance disappeared. And I believe you are talking about the *Irish* Travellers. They can be a cantankerous lot, admittedly. I'm referring to the classic Romani travellers, of course."

Garrick had only been vaguely aware of the difference in Traveller culture until that very morning. Peter Thorpe's comment about Jamal finding shelter amongst them had been bothering him all night. If she'd been accepted amongst them, and taken by their kindness so much that she was even dreaming of going to bat for them in court, then why hadn't *anybody* come forward to report her missing? As usual, a call to John had proved to be a useful source of background information. Although it cost him an over-priced cream tea.

John applied the cream before the jam as he lectured Garrick. "They're heathens, all of them. I don't have time for them. Bunch of thieves and drunkards."

It surprised Garrick to hear such strong opinions from the normally placid man.

"What have they ever done to you?"

"I told you, we had a bunch passing through here before Christmas. Broke into my car and stole the stereo."

"You didn't tell me."

John examined the first decorated half of the scone. "You were very much otherwise engaged."

His sister. How stupid of him. How could that have slipped his mind?

John continued. "They came through here, littering the place. Stealing anything that wasn't nailed down. They should all be thrown in the Channel with the rest of them."

"How do you know it was them?"

"When they cleared off towards Hawkinge, the crime spree stopped." He bit into the scone and sighed with approval. "Now *that's* traditional." He looked around the café and dropped his voice conspiratorially. "At least she kept the recipe, not that I approve of all this modernisation. The name of this place sounds like something out of that bloody sitcom, *Friends*. Hate it."

Garrick chuckled to himself. John's concept of modernisation extended to the new stools, a long wooden bench that ran the length of the café - allowing customers to sit on either side - improved lighting and, horror of horrors, Wi-Fi. The new proprietor was rushed off her feet, despite the lack of customers, as her waitress was running late. That had meant their cream tea had arrived a whole five minutes later than expected. Another act of sacrilege that had annoyed John.

"You're old before your time, John."

John winked. "I still have my youthful vigour. I just don't understand what this obsession is about updating everything. It's just not needed." He turned to the man in the wax jacket and called over. "Stan, I was just telling my friend here about the trouble we had with the *gypos*."

Stan glowered over his newspaper. It was a free copy of the Metro, Garrick noted. No expense spared.

"Bloody bunch of pikeys. Should all be arrested and rounded up and slung in a camp or something. Sponging on benefits and causing no end of trouble. They tried to break into my sheds and pitch up on my land. Police did nothing! I tell you. Nobody wants 'em here."

John smiled and raised an eyebrow at Garrick, as if proving a point.

"I thought you said they were a much-maligned culture?"

"Doesn't that prove my point? Very maligned. It doesn't mean they don't deserve it. I know if they come back through here there are a number of residents who would certainly take matters into their own hands." He finished the scone in two bites. "They have their own traditions, even their own language. Have you ever heard of *Shelta*?" Garrick shook his head. "It's a mishmash of Irish Traveller Cant and Gammon. And I'm not talking about the meat. It's a *cryptolect*. A secret language designed to keep outsiders out. That's just the Irish. The Romani go one better with their own variants, Vlax, Sinte, Welsh..."

"And I had a problem with Cockney Rhyming Slang."

"Far worse than that. It's even worse than Scouse," he added with a smirk at Garrick's expense. John lathered up on the jam on the other half of the scone before adding a liberal mound of cream. Garrick's stomach rumbled as he watched, but he didn't join in.

"It doesn't sound the right type of environment for an Iraqi refugee to call home."

"Good God, no. They can't tolerate outsiders." He gestured to Stan. "And you think Mr BNP is bad?"

Garrick surreptitiously glanced at Stan. He had him pegged as a friend of Farage, but the British Nationalist Party or even National Front seemed a step too far. Nevertheless, he knew the quaint backwaters and idyllic nooks of the Garden of England were a breeding ground for homegrown nationalism. He always hated driving through a lovely village and seeing the red Cross of Saint George flying from somebody's garden flagpole. Saint George. The Patron Saint of England, born in Turkey from Greek parents, served in the Roman army, buried in Israel. The proud symbol of all that is English.

"They wouldn't have much tolerance for her. Unless she was pretty. In which case, it would be like throwing the lamb to the wolves."

"So you don't think it's unlikely she would have stayed with them?"

Garrick chewed the scone, savouring every bite. Garrick patiently waited until he finished.

"Not with the Irish, no. But the Romani are a different kettle of fish." John filled his cup with green tea from the metal teapot on the side. He offered it to Garrick, who nodded, and he filled both cups. "People often think of gypsies as Eastern European tinkers, or bandits," he added with a mischievous smile. "Their roots actually hark back to the Indian subcontinent. And some scholars are talking maybe, circa 400 AD. They have a rich culture and they're not very tolerant of outsiders, yet an Iraqi refugee... I could see them taking her in."

"And you said the ones you had trouble with had moved down to Hawkinge?" The town was only a mile north of Castle Hill, if that.

"They've been circling around the region for months. Pitching up in fields and causing farmers no end of trouble trying to shift them. Don't get Stan started again. You'll never hear the end of it. He'd like to throttle them all."

"Because they don't try to integrate?"

John regarded him with a heavy dose of bemusement. "They see themselves as *very* separate people. Humanity likes its neat boxes, doesn't it? Divide by religion, borders, race, gender, even football teams. We can't help ourselves. Only outsiders see them as the same." He looked thoughtful. "Although they do share obvious similarities." He snapped his fingers. "Valentine!"

Garrick sipped his tea. It was so hot it burned his lips. "Sorry, what?"

"We spoke about Valentine's Day last time. Saint Valentine is the Patron Saint of Travellers. Then again, they have a lot of them. Saint Sarah is probably the more revered one."

"They're a religious people?"

"The ones here are predominantly Catholic. The church is always running outreach programs to help them."

"Guiding Hands," Garrick mumbled.

"Pardon?"

"Nothing." He put his tea down. "Funny, but I always associated gypsies with fortune tellers, the dark arts, and all that kind of stuff."

John shrugged. "Naturally, such a nomadic people pick up a lot of pagan bits and bobs on the way." He rolled his hands together. "Blending it all together. That is what makes them exceedingly superstitious. And there are tales of... darker beliefs."

"Such as?"

"Shaktism. It's a Hindu thing. I read a little. Something to do with Kali. It can involve animal sacrifice. As I say, a rich culture. But a bunch of barmy beliefs. I believe there are some key dates around November for that sort of thing."

Something John had said initially passed him by, but it suddenly came back to him.

"You said people think of them as Eastern European."

"There are substantial communities there, but I was merely pointing out people's generally incorrect assumptions."

"What about Romania?" Discretion meant that he hadn't told John any of the details regarding the investigation, and John knew better than to ask. John's frown prompted him further. "Romanians-Romani...?"

John raised his hands up. "You are meowing up a confused tree." He seemed to take pleasure in Garrick's bewilderment. "They are two incompatible comparisons, sorry. It's merely a linguistic quirk."

The research had overwhelmed Garrick's train of thought. Suddenly, ideas and thoughts that hadn't quite coalesced now fizzled just beyond his reach. He was certain that understanding Jamal's life with these people was critical.

Garrick glanced at his phone, expecting to see dozens of messages. There was only one from Wendy, telling him she was looking forward to their dinner. He had clean forgotten about that and felt guilty for doing so. It was set for early evening, which somehow didn't feel like an actual date, and they had yet to fix a location. For a moment he considered cancelling it, as his mind wasn't in the right space. Besides, there was a very real chance he may have to do just that if the investigation got back in gear. It was seductively easy to post-pone their dinner. It would be a pre-cancellation... but where would that end? He had to remind himself why he signed up to *HeartFelt* to begin with.

Sheer crushing loneliness because his life was all work.

He had to break that cycle, and so far he'd had one date last year with a woman called Sandra, and he'd ruined that.

There were no messages from the team. That meant they had made no tangible progress. He had instructed Fanta to continue chasing her digital footprints, and Chib had taken a search team back to Castle Hill to look for any other clues to what Jamal had been doing there. With more snow overnight, the chances of finding any forensic smoking guns were low, but they had to try.

Garrick found himself staring at Stan. The man caught him and glared back with piggy eyes. Garrick finished his tea.

"So John, these Romani travellers around here. How do you fancy joining me on a little research trip?"

The smile never left John's face. "Oh, no, dear boy. I would absolutely loathe that. I don't mingle with the great unwashed unless I can absolutely help it."

Booking a table for that evening at The Tickled Trout while on his way out of Wye, Garrick then drove to Hawkinge. The snow was coming down in occasional heavy flurries, painting the farmers' fields and distant hills with pristine white charm and crowning the trees with pale halos. It was a beautiful image, but it brought with it an uninvited image of his sister stranded in the snow, somewhere in the wastelands of America. Had she experienced the same feelings of a snowy wonderland before someone had snuffed the life from her?

Garrick was thankful for the slow, grim traffic on the M20. Moving at just under fifty through the salt and sludge carriageway allowed him to focus on something other than his own tortuous inner thoughts. He called the office and asked Harry to find out exactly where the Romani travellers were. It only took him two minutes to call back after he found a plethora of recent complaints to the local police about the Traveller community.

From the sounds of it, Garrick was about to drive into a war zone.

14

The country lane, a quarter mile southwest of Hawkinge, was proving tricky to navigate in the snow. Despite an inch or two elsewhere, here it had drifted, providing thicker coverage, and the narrow lane was well beyond the reach of the gritters.

It pleasantly surprised David Garrick that his shabby Land Rover's four-wheel drive was working as it slipped doggedly onwards. There were signs that a couple of vehicles had passed, but not the large amount he had assumed from a Traveller community. After several minutes of struggling down the lane, he was thinking Harry had been relying on dated information, had it not been for the fact that at the very bottom of the lane he was on now, ended at Crete Road. The very road Jamal had ended her car journey on after leaving the Truckstop. It was too much of a coincidence to ignore. Had Jamal called somebody from the Romani community to pick her up and take her home? As to why they had stopped at Castle Hill, a good mile from the reported Romani site, he wasn't clear.

Garrick craned forward in his seat as the trees to the left cleared, and he spotted several vehicles parked in a snowy field. Four horses ambled around the site, blankets tied over them for warmth.

He stopped when the view over the hedge lowered enough for him to see about twenty caravans, some in better condition than others, yet all carried a slight air of dilapidation. Most were positioned in an approximate circle, reminding him of Old West pioneer wagons. Several had been parked further out, like strays banished from the group. Each was accompanied by either transit vans or estate cars. Smoke rose from a bonfire at the centre of the ring, around which the entire community gathered. Men, women, and children.

Crawling a little farther up the lane, Garrick stopped at a gate that, although closed, bore all the hallmarks of having been forced open. He climbed out, pulling his Barbour tight and kicking himself for not having the forethought to bring a pair of gloves. As he clambered over the fence, he noted there were no footprints or tyre tracks leading from the field.

Fresh snow crunched underfoot, and within seconds the damp had seeped through his sensible shoes and his socks were wet. He stumbled on the frozen, furrowed earth beneath the snow. He couldn't be any less prepared for a countryside ramble.

The smell of burning wood filled his nostrils, and with it, the sound of raised voices. Three people were having a heated argument in a tongue he didn't recognise. A small, dark-faced girl spotted him first. She pointed and, with a sharp few words, the entire group turned his way and fell into silence. They didn't move or make even the slightest gesture of welcome. Their expressions were deadpan, neither hostile nor friendly.

Garrick took his hands out of his pockets and smiled in what he hoped was a friendly manner, even though his teeth were chattering and his toes frozen.

"Hello." He nodded at several of the elders, hoping one of them was some sort of leader. Sharp crackles from the bonfire and the crunch of snow underfoot were the only sounds. Not even the birds sang.

He counted fourteen children, no older than twelve. All carried a slightly grubby air and wore clothes that didn't quite fit, and were certainly not suitable for the cold. Six teenagers glowered, exchanging quick glances at their elders as if expecting to be instructed into action. A majority of the adults were no older than middle-aged. He estimated the oldest woman to be in her sixties. As he drew nearer, he saw two young women cradling babies, one of which cried. The women couldn't be more than twenty.

He stopped six feet short of the elder woman and repeated his hello in case she was hard of hearing. No, apparently she just wasn't interesting in engaging with him. Now he was close, he could see subtle Indian characteristics; a soft cappuccino complexion with dark hair and wide, brown eyes.

"My name is David. I wondered if I could ask you a couple of questions?"

No answer was forthcoming as an additional layer of suspicion descended. Garrick had no choice but to tell them what he was, but knew the moment he mentioned 'police' that if he wasn't tossed on the bonfire, then he'd certainly be shown to the gate. He needed a little damage control to pave the way. He gestured around the field.

"I'm not here about the field, or anything. As far as I'm

concerned, you're welcome to stay." Not strictly true, but he needed them onside. "So I come as a friend." He mentally kicked himself. He was now sounding too much like some old Wild West sheriff speaking to the native Indians. "I'm a police detective." He noticed a slight shift in the crowd. People were tensing, their guards descending even further. He held his hands out and broadened his smile and spoke faster. "But please don't think that makes me a complete bastard. I'm actually trying to help your community."

"We don't need no help, sir." It was the older woman who spoke. Her tone was low and surprisingly friendly, although no smile backed that up.

"I'm sure you're more than capable of solving your own problems, but this is about somebody who needs help from the outside." He took his phone out and selected the best picture he had of Jamal. "I know this girl was living with you."

The moment he held it up, the woman's brow knitted in an unmistakable sign of sorrow. It was fleeting, but definite. Garrick shivered as the snowfall increased. He wasn't in the mood to try to gently loosen tongues, and subtlety had never been his forte.

"She was an Iraqi refugee over here illegally, but I don't care about that. I am investigating her murder." His voice carried over the crowd, but other than the crackle of flames, there was no response. That meant they already knew.

"I know she found solace here and spoke highly of you." It ran against his instinct to give so much information away, but he had no choice. "We have two suspects in custody."

He moved the phone so that everybody could see. Her image stirred reactions from several men, and dark looks were exchanged amongst some of them.

"I have no interest with the folks over there," he gestured towards the town, "who may have a problem with you setting up camp here. I don't care about them. I care about her. My sole interest is in bringing her killer to justice, and I have little time. I said I was here to help you, the truth is, I am asking for your help."

He put the phone back in his pocket and kept his hands there too, as his fingers felt numb. The wind kicked up, blowing eddies of snow across the camp, and causing the fire to pop and crackled fiercely. Still nobody spoke and Garrick didn't know what he should do next, other than turn around and return to the warmth of his car.

Finally, the woman spoke up.

"You have come at a bad time. We have had a death." She gestured to a caravan parked the furthest from the others.

"I'm sorry to hear that."

"How we deal with death differs from you, sir."

"I apologise. I don't mean to be insensitive, but the investigation really can't wait."

The woman gave a curt nod. "And I reckon it'll be no good you freezing to death standing there. It doesn't say a lot about Romani hospitality, does it?" She turned and barked a few words at the crowd. A pair of wooden stools appeared close to the fire. A mug of brown tea was thrust into his hand. The rest of the community disappeared like smoke in the wind.

The woman pulled a shawl tighter around her neck and gestured to the fire.

"Sit by the *yog*. Let it take the chill."

He sat down, luxuriating in the waves of heat. The woman joined him. Up close, he could see her skin was smooth, making her look far younger than she was. Streaks of grey ran through her wavy black hair, and she was just as attractive now as she must have been two decades ago.

"David?"

"DCI David Garrick. And you?"

"Kezia."

"This is your community?"

"My husband's. But he is not here."

Garrick sipped the tea as he waited for her to elaborate. It was extremely sweet, with a syrupy thickness he hoped was honey. Whatever it was, it kissed his throat and warmed him to the bones. When no further explanation was forthcoming, he pressed on.

"Tell me about the girl."

Kezia folded her hands over her lap and eyed him thoughtfully. "Jamal became part of our community, despite being a *gadji*. Folks took a shine to her, and she worked hard."

"Do you often help refugees?"

Kezia shook her head fiercely. "We have problems of our own, without inviting them from others."

"What work did she do?"

"There are always jobs to be done," she replied cagily. "And she never complained."

"Tell me how she came here."

"September last. We was out Hythe way, and she was half starved. Manfri found her. He's a soft heart, that lad. Despite what you hear about us, we're not animals. Especially when it comes to leaving a pretty young *rakli* to her fate."

"Forgive my ignorance, but don't you people travel across the country? Hythe to here isn't much of a journey."

She shrugged. "Maybe it is time to move on."

"So she stayed with you?"

"She stayed with Manfri."

"Her boyfriend?" He was quickly learning that uncovering details was going to be like extracting teeth.

Kezia chuckled. "That he would think himself, for sure. Marriage is the way with us, but Jamal was maybe too strong-minded for that."

Garrick looked around. There was no sign of anybody, yet he got the distinct impression he was being watched. "May I speak with Manfri?"

"When he returns, you might."

"Where has he gone?"

"I told you this is not a good time, sir. It is Manfri's tata who died." She indicated the far caravan again. "Manfri was afraid, so he's gone."

Questions queued up in Garrick's mind, but each one would need to be fished out with patience. He sipped his drink and made appreciative noises.

"I'm sorry to hear that. How did he die?"

Kezia tapped her heart with a balled-up fist. "This stopped dead. Duke was never shy of shouting his opinions to whoever would listen, and most who didn't want to. He held some influence here..." Whatever those opinions were, she stopped herself from explaining.

"What is Manfri afraid of?"

"*Marimé.*" She tilted her head as she assessed him. "We have a certain understanding of death. It's impure, a stigma. And when it graces a family, the impurity becomes infectious. That is marimé. We don't bathe until after the funeral. And you don't touch the body until they're laid below. Lest they come back."

Garrick followed her gaze to the caravan and now understood why it had been moved aside. The body must still be there, threatening to spread its curse across the community. John had warned him they were a superstitious lot.

"I understand. So Manfri is trying to avoid a similar fate."

"Aye. And he's also tasked with arranging the funeral." She said that with a slight smile, which was broadened by Garrick's embarrassment. "He'll be buried Monday afternoon. Over there." She tilted her head in the direction of the village. "A proper catholic burial, mind. That's when you can see him."

"Monday? I'm afraid I can't wait that long." A whole weekend was a lifetime for the investigation.

"Nevertheless, that's when you'll see him. That's when I'll catch him, too."

"Does he have a phone?" She shook her head. "Do you have a photograph? I can put a search out for him. We need to speak with him about Jamal." Kezia firmly shook her head. Garrick bit back his frustration. It wouldn't help to start an argument.

As if sensing that, Kezia gently touched his knee and looked him straight in the eye. "Manfri is a good lad, sir. If he runs when he sees you coming, it's because he's trying to protect you. Death follows him."

It was a matter-of-fact statement. She removed her hand.

"When did he last see Jamal?"

"You'll have to ask him. I saw her that morning. As bright a thing as ever."

"Did she have plans for the day?"

"The usual," she replied vaguely. She stared at the flames, then finally continued. "She was excited about moving on."

"You were all moving?"

"Moving on with her life. She had sought asylum."

"At the risk of being deported if it didn't happen?"

"I said as such. I didn't want to see that happen. She could always stay here as one of us."

"Manfri must not have been happy about her decision?"

Kezia's gaze didn't stray from the flames. Once again, Garrick gave himself a mental kick. She would not be led by such clumsy questions, and his technique was rusty. He quickly changed tact.

"Did she have any friends or work colleagues outside the community?"

"She spoke with people, I believe. I only know of a lorry driver, the one who bought her over. She had stayed friendly with him." Garrick forced himself to remain calm and took another sip of the invigorating tea.

"She brought him here one time." A look of disgust flashed across her face. "There was a terrible argument..."

"Do you remember his name?"

She nodded. "Mircea. A Romanian. A nasty piece of work."

Garrick's heart skipped a beat. A connection at last. He tried not to let his excitement show.

"But he saved her life surely, by bringing her over."

"He used her."

"How?"

"Manfri wanted to kill him. He was not welcome back."

She lapsed into silence and looked at Garrick. He emptied his cup and had the overwhelming feeling that his time was up. He placed the cup into the snow.

"Thank you for your hospitality and sharing what you know." He stood. Kezia remained seated.

"Jamal may not have been Romani, sir. But she was one of us. Her death has touched us all, and we will all pray that you find who did that to her."

Garrick nodded solemnly. "I intend to. You said she lived with Manfri." He swept his gaze across the caravans. "It would be helpful if I could see where she slept."

Kezia treated him to another one of her long, hawkish silences. Then he followed her gaze to the outlying caravan, and she gave a nod.

"Her, Manfri and Duke lay there. You go in, then I can't speak with you again until after the funeral."

Garrick nodded in understanding. He took a few steps towards the caravan when she called out again.

"I'll pray you find who did this, sir. And you are welcome back when the time is right."

Garrick realised he had, somehow, taken a step over the threshold of, if not acceptance, then certainly tolerance. Before he turned away, another question struck him.

"How did you know Jamal had been murdered?" Her identity had not been revealed to the media.

Kezia gave an enigmatic shrug. "News travels, bad news doubly so. People talk, and we are always listening."

15

There was every chance that the stale scent of death was woven into the fabric of the caravan long before Duke had died. Light struggled through the dirt-encrusted windows and was further tempered by nicotine-stained net curtains. It was cooler inside the cramped space than outside, and Garrick's every breath came in a puff of vapour.

The caravan's layout was much the same as every other one Garrick had stayed in with his sister and parents as they sat shivering on some bleak shingle beach in Wales. That's what had usually passed for a holiday back then. It wasn't designed as a pleasure, but more of a punishment to prevent them from complaining about what little they had back home. It was always a spot in Wales that was bleaker than his native Liverpool. A week was just enough to grind down their enthusiasm and make them all eager to return to their terraced house. Then another year would pass before the threat of another holiday loomed.

They had laid Duke out on the bed, dressed in a suit. He

was over six feet tall and heavyset. Garrick imagined that in life he would have made for an imposing figure. His receding dark hair was tinged with white. They had made no attempt to comb it after death.

Somebody had folded his arms across his chest and there had been little effort to imbue him with fake life, with a mortician's makeover. His skin was as leaden as the walls. Sallow cheeks pulled the side of his lip up in a rictus sneer, as if displaying his contempt for death and revealing teeth stained black and yellow from years of neglect. Garrick noted his hands were overly large, with his fingers laced together. The backs of them were scarred and weather-beaten. There was no jewellery, but pale bands of pinched skin showed every finger had carried at least one for many years. His shoes were polished, indicating he had some pride, although the soles had worn thin. Garrick wondered if that was some cosmic pun on the state of the man's own soul.

The bed took up the back space where a table would normally sit. In the middle was a small bathroom and toilet. Opposite lay a tiny plastic kitchen worktop, sink, and two gas burners. The front of the caravan had a smaller mattress propped up on plastic crates. It could be partitioned by brown shower curtains, which hung limply from a plastic rail on the ceiling. Garrick assumed this was the area where Manfri and Jamal slept. There was scant hope for privacy, and Garrick wondered how the young girl could have felt at home with someone like Duke sleeping mere feet away.

He was viewing that from the luxury of a first-world western eye; he reminded himself. It was already clear that Romani attitudes were very different. And from the point of view of a refugee, this grim caravan was a palace.

There was a distinct lack of personal items. Even the beds

had no blankets, just the bare mattresses which had occasional dark stains that no doubt contributed to the smell. Had Kezia not told him this was the home of three people, he would have guessed that it was an empty caravan used to store corpses. He diligently checked under the mattress. The plastic storage boxes that formed a base were all empty.

The drawers in the kitchen, the cupboards, and the narrow wardrobe space were likewise vacant, expunged of personality and lives once lived.

And drugs.

From the way the caravan had been cleared, Garrick doubted even a skilled forensic team would find a trace of cocaine. And if Jamal had been coerced in to selling it, she would have surely kept such valuable merchandise close.

Garrick was at ease around death. It was all part of the job, yet there was something about the cloying atmosphere that felt creepy. Perhaps compounded by the Romani's superstitions, he was glad to leave.

The snow was falling heavier as he marched back across the site. Kezia had gone and several travellers had emerged once more, standing around the bonfire to soak in the warmth. They eyed him with curiosity, but not hostility. Drinking with Kezia had obviously afforded him some acceptance.

He stopped near a young woman cradling her baby, only belatedly noticing she was openly breastfeeding in the cold. Garrick wasn't such a prude to be shocked, but he was embarrassed that he'd selected her to talk to.

"Excuse me. Kezia told me Manfri and Jamal lived with Duke." He indicated the caravan. That got a nod from the woman. He saw through an open door of the woman's own trailer. It was crammed with personal effects. "Where are their things? Their personal possessions? I didn't see any."

The girl's gaze slid to the bonfire. Garrick wondered what he had said that deserved to be ignored. Then he noticed some things had just been added to the fire. As he watched, flames consumed the sleeve of a jacket. A box and a wooden picture frame were destroyed in seconds. And he realised she had answered him.

"You've burned them?" he asked incredulously.

The woman gave a small smile. "As is tradition. The dead don't need them now, and the living won't touch them."

With a sinking feeling, Garrick watched the flames swatting falling snowflakes as they destroyed evidence of Jamal's life with the Travellers.

16

Garrick's investigations with the Romani Travellers had offered nothing more than tantalizing hints. Jamal had stayed with them, but any evidence of her time there had been erased. That only left Manfri as a direct line of information about her relationship with the Romani, and he had fled, fearing the repercussions of passing the taint of death on to the others. Or at least that was a convenient excuse to go into hiding.

On the drive back to the incident room, Garrick had contemplated officially bringing in the Travellers for questioning, but suspected they would clam up and that would shatter the fragile trust he'd established. Kezia had told him Manfri would surface for the funeral on Monday afternoon. It wasn't too long to wait... and yet...

Instead, he put out a request on the radio for any officer who encountered a young Romani man to let him know. Without a description, it was an impossible ask, but he was clutching at straws.

Mircea had visited the Traveller's community, and something had occurred that made him unwelcome. Did they resent the fact he was forcing Jamal to sell drugs? Had she been trying to extricate herself from her debt to him and using the Travellers' support? Again he felt the answers lay with Manfri.

Kezia had used the term *gadji*. It had taken him a little time on the internet to discover that meant 'non-Romani'. She had been adamant that they rarely helped others, so he was at a loss about how the first victim could also be connected to the community.

He was in the office kitchenette waiting for the kettle to boil as he filled DS Okon in. She'd been forced to call the search off mid-morning because of the increasing snowfall. Under the snow, they had found a patch of bloodstained grass, indicating substantial bleeding, but it didn't match Jamal's.

Back in the incident room, she had decided to run through both Thorpe's and Mircea's statements to see if she could uncover any discrepancies. They had both been annoyingly consistent.

"Without Manfri, we are going nowhere," he sighed.

Chib was only half-listening. "We only have her word for how Duke died."

"What?"

"Duke. Heart failure. Let's throw some baseless accusations against the wall and see what sticks. He was angry at his son for shacking up with a... what did she call her?"

"*Gadji.*"

"You said they are traditionalists, so maybe that really irked him."

Garrick picked up the kettle and poured the water over

the matcha green tea bag in his mug. "So he argues with his son."

"Or he argues with her? A man of his status in the community doesn't want the others overhearing this family argument..."

"So they do it a short walk away. On Castle Hill."

"Something happens. He tries to kill her in a fit of passion, and she runs. He follows. Kills her."

Garrick replaced the kettle and began stirring the tea. He stared at the wall, imagining her hypothesis playing out.

"Wonderful. Perfect. And completely without evidence."

"It might explain why Manfri really went into hiding?"

Garrick nodded. "And the entire community is covering it over."

Chib shrugged. "We'll never know without an autopsy on Duke."

"And we'll never have an autopsy without reasonable suspicion. And no, before you suggest it, we're not going to exhume the body and do one on the side."

"The thought never crossed my mind, sir." It clearly had.

Garrick hid his smile. He was beginning to understand Chib's unconventional thinking. She's going to go far.

"None of that explains why she went straight from Peter Thorpe to Castle Hill, with drugs she didn't want to sell. And we have a chasm about what connects the two victims. Other than our trucker friend being close to both incidents, and the skin being cut from them."

"I have been thinking about that. What if they're not connected?" Garrick continued stirring his tea and prompted her to continue. "Two separate murders, except the second one is a copycat to throw more confusion on the investigation."

It was a theory he hated, but it was the one that had the most merit. If true, that would mean there were *two* killers out there.

"Both our suspects' solicitors are demanding we release them if we're not pressing charges."

"They can wait until Monday."

"If we really don't press charges, then..."

"Then holding them for the full ninety-six hours will bite us in the arse, I know. But that gives us to the end of the day Monday. Just after the funeral, if Manfri decides to show up." He saw the look on her face. "What is it?"

"Interviewing a witness immediately after he's buried his father... I can't think of worse timing."

Garrick gave a humourless smile. "I know. Interviewing him straight after he's murdered his father would be better. That is, if your wacky idea had merit. So it'll be a race against time. But that's Monday's problem, not today's. What else have we got?"

"Something to cheer you up, sir. Noel Johnson. The student who ran from you. DC Lord is interviewing him now."

Garrick hurried to the interview room, forgetting to take the bag out of his cup. By the time he reached the room and sipped his tea, it was stewed and tasted bitter. He stood with Chib in the room outside, watching Harry and Noel over the webcam. A middle-aged woman was acting as the kid's solicitor.

"...That's a lot of money, Noel," said Harry as he made notes.

"That's why I was doing it." There was an arrogance in the student's reply. From the way he had fled the scene, Garrick had expected him to be plea-bargaining for his life.

"And you kept a list of everybody you sold to?"

"I am studying Business A-level," he replied indignantly.

"He thinks himself as a regular Tony Soprano," Chib muttered.

"I would like to see those lists."

"I bet you would." Noel gave a derisive snort.

"He's a regular little shit, is what he is," Garrick replied.

"And Peter Thorpe supplied you with everything?"

"Yep."

DC Lord seemed to have run out of steam with his questioning. With a sigh, Garrick marched into the room.

"Don't get up." Nobody had been about to. He took some satisfaction in seeing a tremor of uncertainty cross Noel's face when he recognised him.

Garrick sat down, nursing his mug in both hands.

"Let the record show that DCI Garrick has joined the interview," Lord said, a little put out that his boss had stolen the limelight.

"How many other monkeys did Thorpe have running around?"

The question threw Noel.

The solicitor spoke up, and Garrick now remembered her from a past case. He also remembered that she hated him. "Detective, I must object to the term monkey."

"I object to your client selling class A-drugs on my turf, so it just goes to show you can't always get what you want." He stared at Noel. "I know he had others who were turning over far more than you."

That annoyed Noel. Good. Time to wind him up.

"I bet he even had students doing a degree in Business." Garrick extended his little finger. "You are this guy here. Small fish in the shark tank. Fish food. Oh, there was this girl..." Garrick rolled his eyes around the room, searching for her name. "Foreign sounding..."

Noel's cheek twitched in anger. "Jamal? She was a stupid cow he kept around because he was screwing her!"

"Oh. Well, if you say so..." Garrick leaned back in his chair and played nonchalant. "He told me she could sell cocaine to Eskimos. I'm surprised he didn't get you both working together."

Noel shrugged. "I met her a few times when he was handing me the merch. She was fit, but stupid. I work better on my own."

Garrick smiled encouragingly. "I see. She didn't go for your charm. They can be like that."

Noel nodded in agreement. "Exactly."

"When was the last time you saw her? We're trying to find her."

"Couple of weeks ago." He shrugged and picked at the table to show he was bored with the questions.

"Where did you do these hand-offs with her?"

"Always some place quiet and out of the way. Usually up at Castle Hill."

Garrick's gaze bored into him.

"Is that a fact?"

Garrick was once again fizzing with excitement when Noel was taken to his cell. He unleashed his train of thought on Chib and Harry outside the interview room.

"We have linked Thorpe and Jamal to Castle Hill, and we have Mircea and Jamal at the Traveller camp. Both suspects are connected to key places of interest, reported by witnesses."

"Neither of them were anywhere near Castle Hill that night."

"Their phones weren't. They were safely tucked up in bed. Doesn't mean they were."

"I asked around Thorpe's apartment block," Harry said. "Nobody saw him coming in or out. So he has no witnesses to confirm he was there."

"What did the apartment search throw up?"

"No sign of drugs, but a hundred and thirty quid in cash. There was nothing at the Truckstop either. He was smart enough to keep the illegal stuff out of his hands."

Chib sighed and shook her head. "It makes no sense for Thorpe to give her the package, then race to stop her selling it. And Mircea didn't leave his truck..."

Garrick decided it was time to call it a night before he fell victim to further disappointment.

The snow had abated, so the drive home was under a crystal clear sky. Travelling down the quiet B-roads, the Land Rover baulked on a few black ice patches, but he kept it slow and steady so he could enjoy seeing the stars stretch from one horizon to the other.

Once more his mind's eye catapulted him to Illinois, and the night his sister was murdered. Had she been looking out on a similar vista, under an endless canopy of stars? He could only imagine such parallels. And for whatever reason, on that drive home, he felt her loss more than he had in weeks. He put it down to the fact his own case was getting under his skin.

The more intricate a picture he built of Jamal's life, the more her death sank its claws into him. She was a refugee. Other than the Romani, there was nobody to feel her loss. Who was going to mourn for her? Was he subconsciously assigning that task to himself?

The same applied to Galina, the poor girl they'd found

last year. Except he still hadn't built a profile on her life, so his professional detachment was still intact. Nobody had come forward to claim her, either. Even the Romani didn't seem to know about her. She was truly a lost soul. Two innocents cut from a world that had never cared for them, and never would.

After a shower, he still had plenty of time to make it to his date. He turned on the TV and checked the post. There was some junk mail and a letter from the NHS reminding him of his appointment Monday morning. A good thing too, he'd put his MRI out of mind. And with any luck, he'd forget about it in the morning, too. He didn't want his weekend taken up worrying about something he had no control over.

He switched the television off as the title sequence of a new cop show started. It was the rating's grabber everybody was talking about, so naturally Garrick had no desire to watch it. He sat at the kitchen table and laid open the book he'd bought from John: *The Art of Fossil Preparation*. There was a heavy academic preface he quickly scanned through, but moved to the illustrated pictures showing the best techniques to air scribe the fossil from the surrounding rock matrix. The rock in question was one he had found on the beach on the north coast of the Isle of Sheppey after a storm last December.

He'd gone for a walk to take his mind off his sister. Ordinarily it was a place he enjoyed exploring, with views of the North Sea, across to the Red Sands Fort – massive concrete structures rising from the water on spidery legs, as if they were some alien war machines landing on earth, rather than the remnants of Maunsell Forts built during the Second World War to protect the Thames Estuary. One had even washed up on the beach; an enormous concrete house that provided a surreal play area for adventurous children.

He often found fossils here. Usually uninteresting ones. On this occasion, he had found the distinctive spiral shell of a mollusc poking from the rock. An inch in diameter, he could already see some exposed detail. It was the most marvellous thing he had ever found.

Since then, he hadn't dared touch it until he had both the correct equipment and technique to extract it in one piece. His air pen, a handheld stylus that used compressed air to chip away the matrix, had only arrived two weeks earlier. Now he had the methodology to use the equipment laid out on the pages in front of him.

He put on a pair of protective goggles and started the air pen. It buzzed to life like a dentist's drill. Angling a mounted magnifying glass, he began the delicate work of freeing his prize.

An hour flew by. Progress had been painfully slow, yet he'd removed a small section of matrix, and a little more of the black spiralling shell had been revealed. After five hundred and forty million years, evidence was finally surfacing. He was losing himself in the task so much that, when he glanced at the time, he realised he would be late for his date.

17

"A policeman? Now, should that make me feel nervous?"

"Only if you have a guilty conscience," Garrick said with a chuckle, and immediately regretted it. What a pompous moron he must sound. His date dutifully smiled, but she didn't take him up on the leading question. "Detective, actually," he added, before realising that sounded desperate.

Wendy pulled a little face, pretending to be impressed, then sipped her wine before quickly putting it down.

"I should make that last," she blurted.

She thinks I'm going to arrest her for DUI, he thought with a sinking feeling. He glanced at his watch. He had been fifteen minutes late, they were only thirty minutes into the date, and it was a train wreck already.

You shouldn't have looked at your watch...

"It's not as exciting as it sounds," he added, taking a longer sip of wine, and aware that she had not opined whether or not being a detective sounded exciting. "What is it you do?" he added hurriedly.

Wendy didn't look quite like her profile picture, but who did? She was a tad bigger than the action-hiking profile suggested, but in a very good way. With straight blonde hair past her shoulders, and round blue eyes that sparkled with curiosity. Her face was a little fuller, but better for it, too. She kept reaching for her hair to comb back a lock.

She worked in a school as a teaching assistant. Her hands moved animatedly as she described the problem kids, but countered that by laughing about the joy the job brought when she could help them. Work was clearly the focus of satisfaction in her life, and Garrick related to that. He listened with encouraging nods as she talked in a quick, nervous patter. She never had the patience to train as a teacher and thought that she was probably not clever enough.

By the time Garrick had seen the window to throw in a complimentary, *"I'm sure you are,"* she had already moved on.

She'd had her heart set on becoming the school librarian, but when the staff member announced his retirement, the school's short-sighted headmaster made the decision that the twenty-first century didn't require libraries any more. So while she loves her job and the rest of the staff, she now feels penned in, with no opportunities for promotion or expansion.

She took another nervous sip of wine before ploughing on.

"That had been a wake-up call, really. A realisation that my life was in a rut. Well, not a rut, but certainly on a single track going forward. Replaying the same routine over-and-over again. So I thought, if I can't change my job, I shall have to change everything else."

She was no longer looking at Garrick, but glancing out of the window, unloading a stream of consciousness that he suspected had been bottled up for some time.

"I'd had a few serious relationships, but lately they veered towards other members of staff and in such a tight team, things get awkward." She finished her wine, clinging to the glass like a life preserver. "So it was something of a relief to escape and see what was on offer online. Another change of scene!" She held up her empty glass, and Garrick lifted his to clink it.

Finally, he had a way into the conversation. "My sister forced me to sign up online. I know what you mean about dating people in the same profession. I've always been in the force. Never date a copper." He added, before wondering if he was subconsciously self-sabotaging his date.

"Your whole life? Wow. That's a serious commitment. Before the school, I used to be a commercials manager for KMFM. That was a tough gig. I didn't sell the commercials. I was effectively selling chunks of radio silence that would be later filled with commercials." Garrick nodded but said nothing, which broadened Wendy's smile. "Yeah. Just like that. I could have parked an advert for a car dealership in there." She nervously went to take a sip of wine before remembering the glass was empty. Garrick sipped his, prolonging the uncomfortable silence. He glanced out of the window. Had the beer garden not been blanketed with snow, there would have been a delightful little waterfall outside as the Great Stour flowed past. Instead, the view was bleak.

They were saved when the waitress came to take their order. They both skipped the starters and went for the main course. Wendy chose a chicken salad while Garrick went for the blue cheeseburger and chips. He was no longer feeling sophisticated, so any pretence to impress Wendy had jumped out of the window.

The small talk as they waited for the food was just as awkward as they discussed family. Or rather, Garrick listened as Wendy told him about her sister, retired parents, and an assortment of eccentric aunts and uncles. Garrick had nothing to say about his own family, so he was relieved when the server interrupted to ask if they wanted more drinks. Wendy pointedly ordered sparkling water instead of another wine.

The food came, and the conversation switched to hiking. Wendy was keen on outdoor exercise and part of a local rambling group, which seemed to be how she spent most of her free time. They were nearing the end of the main course when she asked Garrick about his interests. He thought long and hard before answering.

"I enjoy finding fossils and cleaning them."

Wendy's smile didn't flinch, but she hadn't been expecting that answer. Garrick wished the ground would open up and drop him in the Stour. When it came to dessert, neither of them had an appetite.

Garrick offered to pay the bill, but Wendy insisted on paying half, reminding him it was the twenty-first century. An awkward handshake in the car park they parted just as it began to snow again, with half-hearted promises that they should '*do that again*'.

Garrick wasn't sure his pay cheque could stretch to such an overpriced burger more than once per month.

Driving home, he interrogated himself over the disastrous lunch. What had he been thinking? Wendy was an attractive, articulate woman, while he struggled to be monosyllabic. If anything, it showed him how dull his life had become. Wendy had been right about shaking things up. He needed to do the same.

He needed a break in the case.

He drove towards Ashford as he thought about what they may have overlooked at the Ashford Truckstop. That was the one location placing Jamal with the two suspects at the same time, but just not physically *together*.

There was a piece missing in the jigsaw.

The wind whipped the snow when he arrived. Garrick showed his ID card to the security guard at the gate and parked up. It was almost filled with trucks from across Europe. He strolled over to where Mircea had parked his lorry, on the far side of the car park and directly opposite the restaurant building, affording him a full view of everybody coming and going. He'd backed into a berth, his cab facing out with the doors to his trailer snug against the perimeter fence.

Garrick recalled the security footage in his mind. He pictured Jamal climbing from the cab and walking five-hundred feet across the carpark, into the restaurant.

What was he missing? It was a clear path. They had footage of Jamal entering the site. Climbing into the lorry and then, forty minutes later, heading to the restaurant before leaving.

Forty minutes in which she was alone with Mircea in his cab. What had they been doing? Mircea claimed she was a prostitute, but Thorpe was adamant that the lorry driver was gay. The girl had no signs of recent intercourse.

Thorpe claimed she had been pleading with Mircea to let her go free, while he subjected her to threats of turning her in to immigration. But hadn't she already decided to turn herself in? That would effectively rob Mircea of any hold he had over her. Why would Thorpe lie?

Garrick traced Jamal's steps towards the restaurant. Had she told Mircea that she would no longer do his dirty work? If so, there had been no signs of a struggle in the cab. And if she had done so, why did she then enter the restaurant to speak with Thorpe?

If both men knew she was no longer selling his drugs, then why had he given her a parting quantity of drugs to sell? Why had she accepted?

Garrick stopped outside the restaurant and turned back to look at a lorry parked in the same berth the Romanian had used. He stood at a similar angle to the camera footage he'd watched several times over. Jamal opening the cab door, climbing down, and walking towards the building.

Opening the door... climbing out...

Then it struck him as he studied the parked lorry. She had entered and exited on the driver's side of the cab. It was a continental lorry, and likely that Mircea was resting on the sleeping cot in the back. It was also possible to come and go through the passenger door on the opposite side, which the camera was blind to.

Had Mircea actually been in the lorry at the time?

Garrick hurried back to the lorry currently parked there. In his mind's eye, he lined himself up with another camera on a pole in the opposite corner. Parked trucks blocked the view. His team had given him the best footage, but he hadn't seen *everything*... because the cameras couldn't see everything.

He walked to the perimeter fence. It was green plastic-coated metal, woven into a large mesh with holes big enough to fit his fist through. Age and neglect had damaged it. In places the plastic sheath had peeled back, exposing the wire which rusted under the elements. The mesh was slightly crumpled at the bottom. A quick check revealed the same superficial damage right along the fence caused by lorries that had backed too far, tearing the bottom of the mesh from the supporting pole, like folding the corner of a page in a favourite book. Garrick kicked the bottom, and the fence moved freely. He knelt and pulled at it. It easily came away from the floor. He could lift it high enough to crouch under and step into the woods beyond.

A few paces into the woods and the snow came up to his knees, ruining yet another pair of shoes in the process. He used the torch on his phone to light the way. Concealed twigs and branches clawed at his trousers as he pushed between the trees. Twice he fell, swore, and picked himself up. Then he unexpectedly stepped out onto a quiet country road.

The snow hadn't been cleared from Cheeseman's Green Lane, and the tracks of a couple of vehicles showed few people were in a rush to use it. In the middle of the night, it would be deserted.

It would be the perfect way to slip in and out of the lorry park unnoticed.

18

Garrick was surprised to discover Fanta and Wilkes were in the incident room late on a Saturday night. It was close to eleven, and they had both returned home to slip into their civvies before returning to share a takeaway as they ran through their case notes. The day had been damaging to morale. Just as they felt on the verge of making a breakthrough, they had in fact got nowhere, and it grated on the young team's pride. He also had the nagging feeling that he had walked in on a personal moment between them. DC Fanta Liu certainly was unusually reserved.

He glanced at her screen as he passed. She was focusing on Galina.

"I felt sorry for her. As if we've overlooked her a bit too much," she explained.

They had, of course, Jamal was the immediate focus of the investigation and so far, the cases were related only by a few similarities, and if it wasn't for the lead that had been offered by the refugees, then they wouldn't even have her name.

"Anything popped?" he asked, logging into his computer and hanging his coat on the back of his chair.

"Sean and I went to Napier and asked a few more questions."

Garrick cast a look at Sean. "Did you now, Wilkes? That was mighty enterprising of you."

Wilkes didn't look around, but his cheeks flushed with embarrassment.

DC Liu coughed to get Garrick's attention back to the topic. "She was undocumented, like Jamal. It made me think somebody was deliberately picking on them."

"What do you mean?"

"The people on the fringe. The ones who won't cause a stir if they go missing." She shivered at the thought. "Think about how horrible it must be for your death to go completely unnoticed. I hope if I go, you lot will be in deep mourning for months. Maybe years."

"I will be," Wilkes called over from the board, where he was studying the faces of Thorpe, Mircea, and Leon. "Who'll make my coffee, then?"

Fanta crumpled up a printout and threw it at his head. The perfect strike bounced off his ear. She turned back to her boss as if that had been all perfectly normal.

"Something jumped out for me. Apparently, she was a Christian."

Garrick frowned. "I thought she was from Iraq?"

"They have Christians there. But yes, I thought it was surprising. So I was going to suggest we get some uniforms asking around churches. See if anybody recognises her."

Garrick started hunting through the folders of digital

video evidence on HOLMES. Fanta tensed, fearing she was going to be reprimanded for something...

"You better watch your step, Pepsi–"

"Fanta."

"Because if you keep this up, you might get headhunted off my team."

"Maybe they'll remember my name," she muttered quietly. She didn't notice the sly smile tugging Garrick's lips as he played a surveillance video from the truck stop.

Silence filled the room as everybody settled into their own avenues of investigation. After thirty minutes, it was broken by Wilkes offering to make a cuppa for them all. Garrick declined, but didn't take his eyes off the screen.

"Ah-ha! Both of you come here and take a look at this." Fanta rolled her chair over to his desk. Wilkes stood behind her, his hand gently resting on her shoulder – before he remembered himself, and quickly removed it. They watched the video of Jamal exiting Mircea's lorry and walking to the restaurant. "Did you see it?"

Wilkes and Fanta exchanged puzzled looks.

Garrick replayed the video full screen and tapped the truck's windshield. "There, as she exits, the cab light comes on." He played it again to prove his point.

"That's what happens when you have a vehicle that works properly." Fanta had seen the state of Garrick's Land Rover.

"Now watch this."

He selected another video clip and played it. It was the same camera, and Mircea's truck hadn't moved. Nothing happened. Then another truck appeared at the side of the screen as it reversed into a space. At the same time, a pair of drivers exited the restaurant and stood smoking outside in the drizzle.

"Did you see it?"

"See what, exactly, sir?" Wilkes asked.

Garrick tutted and replayed the same section of footage. "Eyes on Mircea's truck."

They saw the cab light come on, then go off seconds later.

"Somebody left the cab," Garrick declared. He played it again. Wilkes pointed to the parking truck.

"I suppose it could be glare from this lorry's headlights on the window." But as he watched, it was obvious it couldn't be that.

"Mircea could have been asleep inside and turned the light on for a moment," Fanta offered.

Garrick stopped the footage as the light came on. It was too far, and the camera quality too poor, to make out details. He wished there was a way to enhance footage like they did on TV, but the plain fact was, if the resolution wasn't there to begin with, there was nothing to enhance.

"Yes, it's possible he turned the light on briefly. But I think he left the cab from the passenger's side. Jamal climbed in on the driver's side. It's a continental cab, don't forget. And he hasn't pulled any curtains across the windows, so the car park floodlights would be shining right in there, so he wouldn't need a light."

He described the broken fence and how it connected to the quiet back road.

"If you're right, then why did she go there in the first place?" asked Fanta. "The door's unlocked. Was he expecting her?"

"It's a secure car park," Garrick said thoughtfully. "So leaving it unlocked... especially if he was expecting her... I can believe that." He scrubbed the footage to the moment Jamal arrived, eighty-seven minutes after the trucker's theoretical exit. "Except when she gets there, intending to tell him she's going to turn herself into the authorities and ask for asylum, he's not there. That robs her of the power she was feeling at that moment. So now she waits inside, alone. But he doesn't come back."

Again, he scrubbed forward to the footage of Jamal exiting the cab and froze the image.

"So she didn't have the argument she expected, and she feels cheated. Upset. She goes to see Thorpe and tells him. Then she's off, maybe doing one last run for Thorpe. Meanwhile, Mircea is already out and about. He has the time to get to Castle Hill and kill her."

Fanta held up her hand. Garrick sighed.

"You don't have to do that."

"I just wanted to point out that if Mircea had slipped out onto the back road, it's still a hell of a walk to get anywhere."

"Unless he was meeting somebody who had wheels," Wilkes said.

"Bloody hell," Garrick murmured.

That meant they had either an accomplice missing from the picture, or an essential link was missing from their chain.

He left Fanta reviewing the rest of the footage, waiting for the cab light to come back on to signal Mircea's return. In the meantime, he took the Romanian into the interview room and had to wait a good ninety minutes for his solicitor and translator to arrive so he could begin. The solicitor made noises about such a late interrogation. Perhaps it was the stress or fatigue, maybe it was the pressure of the case, but Garrick suspected it was because of his lousy date that he cast aside his amiable facade and went straight on the attack.

"I'm a little confused, Mircea. You told me Jamal was a

prostitute. I find that difficult to believe for two reasons. One, what would a gay man want a girl for–"

"You can't speculate on my client's sexuality!" interjected the solicitor.

"I'm sorry, I was merely going from witness statements and the Grindr app he has on his phone."

Mircea's eyes narrowed as he stared at Garrick. "I am both. Bi."

Garrick held up his hands apologetically. "Best of both worlds. Nothing wrong with that. But what's the term for when you're not in your cab at all when your prostitute turns up? Is that tele-sex, or something?" Mircea checked with his translator that he'd heard correctly. It was a handy method to stall for time. Garrick deliberately interrupted and talked quickly.

"You understand me just fine, Mircea, so we can dispense with the theatrics. You knew Jamal was coming to talk to you. You had threatened time-and-time again to notify the authorities that she was here illegally, and when she finally–"

"Please!" cried the translator. "Slow down. I can't keep up."

Garrick was relentless. "He understands just fine, don't you, Mircea? You understand Jamal was going to seek asylum and your hold on her was snatched away. So you did something about it, didn't you? You left before she arrived." He searched Mircea's eyes for any sign of acknowledgement. "Your cab light. It turns on when you open and shut the door. Even when you sneak out the passenger side, away from the cameras, and through the hole in the fence."

There! The cocky bastard's expression flickered for a moment before he composed himself. For the sake of his solicitor and the audio recording, Mircea gave a disparaging snort and leaned back in his chair, folding his arms. He was playing hardball now, but it confirmed everything Garrick needed to know.

Inadmissible as evidence, of course, but enough to put the investigation back on track. Garrick glanced at his phone as a text message popped up from DC Liu. The cab light had flashed again at five in the morning. Enough time for him to murder Jamal and make it back in time for breakfast.

"You must have been so tired that morning. Getting back at what time? Five? And then you were driving all day…"

Mircea's jaw muscles were working overtime as he ground his teeth. Garrick was getting to him and couldn't resist smugly smiling back, although he still didn't have a confession.

Or real evidence.

19

The ringing phone woke him so suddenly that the jolt made him feel sick. Garrick often had to explain why he still had a landline when most people used their mobiles these days. He was tired of explaining that it came with the broadband package, and his mobile reception at home was almost non-existent.

"Yes?" Garrick croaked into the handset. His throat was dry and sore, and he suspected he was coming down with a cold after all his romping through the snow.

"Mister David Garrick, please."

The American accent woke him up instantly. He groped for his mobile and saw it was almost midday, 6am Chicago time.

"Yes. This is me." He rubbed his groggy eyes.

"I hope I'm not disturbing you. This is Sergeant Al Howard from Flora PD in Illinois. USA," he added helpfully.

Now he recognised the voice. It was the same man who had called him up to report the tragic news. It seemed that people called Howard dominated his life. Since then, the good Sergeant had formed a kinship with his transatlantic partner and made sure that Garrick was updated as often as possible. Which had been little over the last month or so.

"No, not at all. I can talk."

"We have a new development." He paused, expecting a reaction, but Garrick knew better than to interrupt. "We discovered an abandoned automobile in Black Oak, Indiana. That's about ninety miles east of us. It had rolled into a ditch, and the snow had pretty much covered it. We're having a real bad winter over here."

Again, he paused. Garrick thought he better give a little "Uh-huh" of acknowledgment, so the Sergeant didn't think they'd been cut off.

"There were traces of blood inside. CSI confirms that it's your sister's and also from one of the other missing victims."

"Where? Where was the blood, exactly?"

Garrick heard the rustle of papers. "Droplets were found in the trunk, but a majority on the backseat. A sign of steady bleeding. Hair and saliva were mostly on the seat."

Garrick pictured the scene. "So she was alive while in the car?"

"Yes. Alive, possibly dying."

"She'd been laid out on the backseat by the sound of it."

"Uh, yes, sir, that is our assessment."

"What about forensic evidence around the car itself? Any idea how many people had been inside? Or where the driver went?"

"David," the Sergeant said patiently, "the automobile had been there for three months now. Between the weather and the way it had been put in the ditch, we were lucky we found it at all. Any forensic evidence around the site will have been destroyed long ago."

"I understand." Although Garrick had known that, he was still irritated that the CSI team hadn't at least tried to search the area. It would have been a waste of time, but it would have at least helped soothe his conscience. "You said the car had been 'put there'? What do you mean?"

"It had a flat tyre. Somebody had tried to fix it until they noticed the spare was flat, too. Then they rolled the vehicle into a ditch and made sure it was pretty well covered. I just wanted to update you on the status, but I'm afraid we don't have any more news than that. We plan to search the area with dogs, but the weather is against us, and I don't think we'll be able to do that for a couple of weeks."

A couple of weeks. Somewhere out there, Emilie's killer was enjoying the extended luxury of freedom. The thought turned his stomach and brought on a pounding headache straight behind his left eyeball. He thanked Sergeant Al Howard for the update and hung up before hurrying to the bathroom for a couple of Ibuprofen and paracetamol to tackle the pain.

It did little to help. A state that would mean his already half-wasted Sunday was going to be a complete washout.

He tried to take on the day by tackling the fossil, which was still on the wooden workboard sitting on the kitchen table. Like his case, yesterday's progress had been quite slow, but what little had been revealed was impressive. He hoped to have time – and the alertness – to remove it from the matrix by the end of the day. Then he could get on revealing the finer detail, which promised to be a lot more fun.

But his mind wasn't playing ball.

The case was becoming a hydra of leads, most of which

would inevitably be false trails and dead ends. His frustration was further compounded by being a mere spectator in his sister's case.

If that wasn't bad enough, he noticed a text message he'd received late last night from Wendy. A simple: *thanks for an interesting dinner. Sorry I was distracted!* A smiley face was the final piece of punctuation.

What the hell did that mean? Should he respond? What could he say? And the fact it would appear as if he'd waited until the next day to reply would look terrible... wouldn't it? The only three women he felt he could ask were all inappropriate for different reasons. Drury was his superior and aloof, even though they'd known each other for years, and he had even been to her house on several occasions for dinner parties. He was only just getting to know Chib, so that felt wholly inappropriate. And asking Fanta was wrong for different reasons. She clearly hated the formality of the workplace, so would probably give him a direct and accurate answer, and then use it against him in a passive-aggressive way when she wanted something from him.

He knew he should go to the incident room, but the complete lack of sleep and the unflinching headache wouldn't enhance his esteem amongst his team. From the emails bouncing around, Chib was already in and up to speed from the previous day's breakthroughs. She was competent enough without him slowing everybody down.

That made him think about his old DS. He still hadn't heard from Eric Wilson since last month and hadn't reached out to him since Drury had told him he'd been seconded up north somewhere. He typed a short email saying that they should catch up soon and sent it into the ether.

The day rolled on and his headache receded. He made

swift progress on the fossil, falling into an almost Zen-like state as he chipped the remaining matrix away. Now he could begin fine cleaning, but the desire to return to the incident room was overwhelming.

It hadn't snowed today, but the temperature was low, aided by a nasty windchill, and his garden was still lost under a white blanket. He fished out his gloves, a long black scarf that had been a present from a favourite girlfriend, and selected a pair of stout walking boots. Then he set off to the incident room, arriving without requiring a single piece of his winter wardrobe.

Chib had left, and there were only Harry and DC Sean Wilkes left.

"Can't keep you away from this place," Garrick said as he passed Wilkes.

"It's overtime, isn't it, sir?"

"I knew there had to be a reason other than upholding justice."

"Well, that doesn't pay as well as the other side, does it?"

Garrick joined Wilkes at the murder wall and stared at Mircea's and Thorpe's pictures, as if they might start uttering confessions.

"Mircea walks the end of tomorrow if we don't get something on him."

"What about Thorpe's confession that he was getting the drugs from him?"

"As much as I hate to say it, it's all circumstantial, isn't it? There hasn't been a whiff of narcotics found on his lorry. He claims that the insulated stowage compartment was there when the company gave him the cab. And it's clean as a whistle. The only forensics they found were Jamal's, and he still claims she was there for sex."

"If he goes to Europe, I reckon he'll go to ground."

"Yeah. I'm afraid so. We have enough on Thorpe to bang him up on Class-A charges."

"Oh, Leon has been singing about that, sir. The NCA wants to talk to them both the moment we sort out the murder charges."

Garrick felt suddenly dizzy. He sat on the edge of a desk and pinched the bridge of his nose as the headache hinted that it was returning.

"But we have nothing that connects him directly to Jamal's murder, or links him in any way to Galina." He pointed at Mircea's picture. "We have to focus on him. Put Thorpe on the back-burner. We have twenty-four hours to find a single piece of evidence to bring him down. We need to get everybody on it."

He was suddenly reminded of his MRI appointment in the morning. With the clock ticking, he couldn't afford to spend the time going down to Tunbridge Wells for it. Then again, could he afford to risk his own health by not going? He was sure Chib was more than capable, but he also knew that if the case fell apart because he was stuck in the hospital, then he'd never forgive himself. It was an unwinnable dilemma.

"We had some responses from the churches," Wilkes said. He caught Garrick's puzzled look. He tapped Galina's picture. "We canvassed a few churches with her picture since she was Catholic. A couple of priests think they recognise her, but since it was over three months ago, none of them can be a hundred percent sure. They say they get a lot of refugees in for mass. They don't ask questions, of course. It's a safe space for them all. They also get gypsies in, too."

Garrick suddenly ignored the pressure between his eyes. "Romani?"

Harry nodded.

"Any particular church?"

"They all get Travellers in, but there was only one fella who thought he recognised Galina, but didn't have a name. He also mentioned the Romani."

Our Lady of Good Counsel was a Roman Catholic church out in Hythe, about five miles from where Galina was murdered. It was a pleasant enough modern, red-bricked building, but the interior was as bland and functional as Garrick expected. He was not a religious man by any stretch of the imagination. Not exactly an agnostic. He often found moments of impromptu belief were thrust upon him when he needed them most. But that was because he preferred to cover all his bases.

Whatever he had been expecting the priest to be like, the skinny thirty-something who was on his hands and knees scrubbing the floor, was not it. The priest bounded to his feet when he saw Garrick and tossed the hard-bristled brush into a bucket of water.

"Good afternoon! The service isn't for another few hours today." He gestured to the pews. "But you are welcome here."

Garrick indicated the large, damp patch on the floor. "I hadn't expected you to be cleaning every inch of the church. That is dedication, Father."

The priest laughed, nudging his round wire-framed glasses up his hawk nose. He had a fuzzy black stubble on his cheeks, and his hair was slicked back. "I'm afraid some people can't handle a little communion. Especially if they have had a little of their own the night before. Or even in the morning."

Garrick was thankful the pungent bleach obscured the smell of vomit.

"I see. I'm not here for..." he waved his hand vaguely towards the font. "I'm DCI Garrick. One of my colleagues asked you about a young woman, a refugee. I'm just following up."

The priest's face transformed to concern, and he wrung his hands.

"Of course. Anything I can do to help. I pretty much told the officer all I could remember. I'm Father Cillian, by the way."

Garrick held up his phone so Father Cillian could see Galina's picture. He peered at it and nodded.

"Yes, I am quite sure she had been here on more than one occasion around October or November. Father McConnell was in charge. He should be here. I'm filling in for him. He has been rather ill, unfortunately."

"Why do you recognise her? You must have many people come through your doors."

"Few of Middle Eastern heritage. She does rather stand out, and she is obviously a refugee from somewhere. We have a few come through our doors, and we are part of a communal outreach scheme that helps them. Guiding Hands."

"I've spoken to Trisha Warren."

Father Cillian's smile brightened. "She is a smashing woman. Whipped up that group out of nothing. Many people depend on her now. They all love her."

Garrick kept his phone up. "Was she part of the Guiding Hands scheme?"

"I personally don't get too involved, but not that I was aware of."

"Do you remember her ever coming with other people? Or did she have friends here?"

Father Cillian puffed his cheeks and expelled a long sigh as he cast his mind back. "Not that I recall. She was a loner. I remember that. I had the sense she was either frightened or nervous. That's another reason I assumed she was here illegally." He held up his hands defensively. "We are not here to make judgments on people."

"Only on their eternal soul," quipped Garrick. The good Father didn't seem to share his sense of humour. "Did you ever speak to her?"

"Of course. I tried several times. I was curious to know where she came from."

"I believe you get a lot of the Traveller community through here, too?"

"The Irish Travellers know they have a safe place here. And I'm Irish myself, so perhaps there is a little bias in me."

"Bias? Towards the Irish... but not towards the Romani?"

Father Cillian's head tilted back as he regarded Garrick with fresh eyes. "Your good officer was asking such probing questions. May I ask why?"

"There is a Romani community currently in the Downs who took a young refugee girl under their wing. Not her." He indicated his phone. "Another."

"As I said, we have all people come here. Irish, Romany, Middle Eastern. What does it matter? We are all God's children."

"Unfortunately, both of these children were murdered."

The gravity of the news struck Father Cillian. He blinked in surprise. "Forgive me. The officer hadn't told me."

Garrick studied him. He looked like a smart fellow, but he wondered why, when he'd been shown a photograph of a woman lying on a morgue slab with her eyes closed, he hadn't made that deduction himself. Admittedly, Garrick had cropped the image to show only her face, so she could pass for sleeping, he supposed...

"That's a tragic shame. Two of them? I wish he'd told me."

"Would that have improved your memory?"

Father Cillian adjusted his glasses again. "Perhaps it would have focused my attention. Disparate questions may make sense to you when seeking answers, but they're of no use helping me offer something that may be of interest to you. You ask about the Travellers in relation to two dead girls, and I can make my own conclusions. And in doing so, maybe recall something useful."

He pressed the knuckle of his index finger against his lips as he sieved through his memories. He paced as something occurred to him.

"She was here when some Romani and a few local folks got into something of a shouting match outside. I'm afraid that a few punches were exchanged. I broke it up." He caught Garrick's dubious expression. "I know I hardly look like Hercules, but fortunately both sides respected the Lord and his servants."

"Was the girl involved?"

"She seemed to be at the centre of it. I'm not sure if she knew any of them, but she was just as much a target as the Romani group. I know she left in a hurry on her own."

"What were they arguing over? Was it drugs, by any chance?"

The priest blinked in surprise. "Good Lord, no! It was about work!"

"Work?"

"The locals were accusing the Travellers, and her of

taking work from them. I know it's the same old story even now after the great Euro uncoupling. Unemployment means that the outsiders get targeted for stealing the jobs that are not there. Between you and me, I can't see any of the local lads picking fruit or getting their hands dirty over some menial back-breaking tasks."

"Who were the locals?"

"I'm not sure of names, but they still come. They are some of the more vocal nationalist members of our community."

"Ah, racists..."

"Let us call them people with precise differences of opinion."

"I call a bigot a bigot, Father. Was this a general lynching, or was it something specific?"

Father Cillian didn't approve of the word 'lynching,' but he let it pass. "It was over some work on a farm near," he stopped to think. "Forgive me. I'm still getting to know the area. It sounded like an Apple."

Garrick was stumped. "Cox? Gala? Pippin?"

Cillian raised his finger. "Braeburn!"

Garrick shook his head until the penny dropped. "Brabourne?"

"Yes, that was it."

Garrick took a card from his wallet and handed it to the priest. "Thank you for your time. If anything else occurs to you, please call me."

"Of course. Good luck."

Garrick slowly walked from the church and out into another bout of light snowfall. He wasn't sure if the priest had offered anything useful, but it helped add a little texture to Galina's life. The link to the Romani was tenuous, but the bigoted behaviour was all too familiar.

His decision about what to do next was answered when his Land Rover, now covered in a sprinkling of snow, failed to start. A call to the RAC had him waiting for recovery. The jolly mechanic told him his battery was knackered. Garrick felt that was an analogy, if ever he needed one, of how he felt about himself.

_____

20

The image of a watch hand, ticking down the seconds, played in DCI Garrick's mind even when he had his eyes tightly closed. It was even more disturbing because the only clock he had looked at all morning was the digital display on his phone.

"Comfortable?" The voice was slightly metallic.

"Yes," Garrick replied without opening his eyes.

"Good. Nice, slow, deep breaths..."

Hell was suddenly unleashed, as if the hordes of the damned were banging metal drums directly down his ears. The pulse from the MRI machine was frightening. He was slightly claustrophobic, so having his head fully inside the machine's metal ring felt like placing it in the guillotine. The heavy rhythmic pulses brought about a sense of approaching dread. Logically, he knew it was a perfectly safe, non-invasive technique, but he also knew that logic crumbled in the face of primal fear. He had seen that many times over his career.

Each sonorous thud seemed to stir his thoughts like a

zephyr through the fragments of his memory. But like fallen leaves, they slipped through his grasping fingers.

After an eternity, silence descended over the room. He lay still, not daring to open his eyes, until a gentle female voice spoke close to him.

"That's it, David. All done."

He quickly dressed and was told the results would be sent directly to his consultant. He had hoped to see them there and then, with a doctor casually pointing out that there was nothing to worry about after all, and the growth was shrinking. Instead, he now faced the uncomfortable wait for a phone call that could be days away.

Following the lines on the floor, Garrick walked to his next port of call for a *phlebotomy*. It sounded sickening enough on the reminder letter he had received, and he wondered why they hadn't stuck with the more understandable word: '*bloods*'. It was hardly likely that the people of Kent would get that mixed up with the violent Los Angeles street gang.

He toyed with his phone, but deliberately kept it switched off. He pretended it was out of respect for the hospital rules, but the actual reason was because he knew that if there was the slightest whiff of a lead on the case, he would be out of the door like a bullet.

He sat on an uncomfortable plastic bucket seat in the small waiting area. It was mostly populated by elderly patients, but a couple of younger faces gave him hope he hadn't yet crested the age hill that led to the one-way slope of the inevitable. The nurse on the station hadn't even looked up when she told him to take a ticket from the small round dispenser bolted on the wall.

He stared at the small, oblong, pink paper. The number

sixty-four was printed in a thick, bold type. With no display on the wall, there was no way to judge how far along he was.

"Forty-eight!" called a male nurse, wielding a clipboard as he waited to see who would stand. An elderly man managed it, leaning heavily on his walking stick. He took small shuffling steps that suggested the waiting time would soon be doubled or tripled.

Garrick stared at the ticket again.

Then he jumped to his feet, holding it out in the palm of his hand as if he'd just won the lottery. He pulled his phone from his jacket pocket and turned it on as he rushed for the exit.

He called Chib first, but she wasn't in the incident room. Fanta, as usual, was at her desk.

"The Galina case. There was a ticket we found on her. A pink one. Did DS Wilson ever find out what it was for?"

He heard the clatter of a keyboard as Fanta checked. Then she started humming.

"The computer is slow today," she reported back.

Aren't we all? He thought. He paced outside the hospital, torn between going back inside or making a dash for his car, which at least had started the first time this morning thanks to the new over-priced battery the mechanic had fitted the previous night.

She came back in her sing-song voice. "Here we go. Nothing fun to report, sir. It was tagged as a bog-standard ticket used for a bunch of stuff, from lotteries to queuing systems."

"So nobody checked hospitals?"

There was a pause. "Well, as a matter of course, they contacted hospitals with her description, but got nothing back. But then again, they didn't have a name. Do you want me to run it?"

"As a priority."

"Okey-dokey."

He hung up, itching to be heading towards some meaningful action. But that wasn't the reality of detective work. It involved hours, days, and weeks of painful inactivity until some clue poked out from the surrounding chaos. He couldn't help but think of his fossil. He was pretty sure he was close to the delicate cleaning stage of solving the case. Everything was there, he thought. Or rather, hoped.

The thrill of his sudden burst of inspiration was already ebbing. It could take Fanta hours or days to get a response. Somewhat sheepishly, he returned to get his bloods taken, only to discover he had missed his number and had to take a new ticket.

He was driving to Hawkinge, aware that time was marching on, and Chib had nothing new to report, when Fanta called back. She had a match. There was a Galina with a patient record at the William Harvey Hospital in Ashford. She couldn't be sure it was the same woman, but with that name, but the odds were in their favour. Not only that, Galina had an appointment the morning before her death. Fanta had insisted that hospital security access the video files to see if they could make a positive identification.

He arrived at the hospital at the same time as Chib, and they made their way inside.

"We have to release Mircea in four hours if we're not formally charging him," she reminded him. "Thorpe's going to be transferred to Maidstone prison. We've got him on the drug charges. He still insists that Mircea is the kingpin. Now our Romanian is claiming Thorpe is just bitter because he wouldn't have sex with him."

"What?"

"A smoke screen, in my opinion. An easy explanation why two men would know one another in a service station. There is no indication that Thorpe is bisexual or gay, but even if he is, we have nothing to nail Mircea for drugs trafficking, other than an empty smuggling compartment in his cab."

Garrick was painfully aware of the pitfalls of releasing him, but also the dangers of holding him with flimsy evidence. If he tried to sue, Mircea's legal team would make mincemeat of the case, leaving Garrick open for accusations of harassment and making it difficult to make further charges stick.

His case was not helped by the fact it hung on the theory that Jamal was *alone* in the Romanian's cab, when in fact the man himself insisted he was there, having sex with her. Few guilty people ever tried to prove to the police that they were in contact with the victim hours before their death.

The phone records proved Mircea was at the Truckstop on the same evenings that both women had been killed. And now that Garrick had discovered the little escape run from the truck compound, he was convinced Mircea was responsible for both, and Thorpe was caught in the middle because of the drug trafficking.

The hospital's Senior Security Officer was a middle-aged Jamaican woman who introduced herself as Brenda. They were still using clunky old video tapes to back up the footage, but she had already pulled the cassettes in question from the archive and had the footage ready at the correct time of Galina's appointment. Garrick couldn't help and admire how proactive and friendly Brenda was, and berated himself for speculating if she was single. Her efficiency was purely down to her excitement about being involved in something more substantial than a parking violation in the car park, rather than Garrick's animal magnetism. But because of her effectiveness, one of the first images they saw was Galina walking towards the main entrance. From the angle she was approaching, Brenda suggested she either lived close by, or had arrived by bus. Taxis and cars usually dropped off outside the door.

Garrick leaned closer to the screen as Brenda switched tapes to show the young woman checking in at the reception desk. She looked the same as he'd found her. Long jet-back hair cascaded either side of her face and ran halfway down her back. Her soft brown skin enhanced her beauty, even as she timidly glanced around the reception. Like Jamal, she looked vulnerable, but that was not the case. Both women had been strong-willed fighters. You didn't make your way across an entire continent using nothing more than your wits without real true grit. He admired that, and doubted he had such resolve himself.

She wore the same baggy jeans and blue coat he had found her in. Too thin for the November chill, an over-sized white jumper poked out from the bottom. He was sure they were taken from a recycling centre; just as he suspected Jamal had obtained her clothing.

They had found Jamal's fingerprints on the clothing dumpster, feet from where she had been killed. They were on the chute's handle, as she had tried to open it. There was no smudging to indicate a struggle, and the evidence pointed to her being attacked from behind as she was trying to claim some drier clothes. Garrick thought back to the night. It had been cold and raining. She had blindly run from Castle Hill, soaked and muddy. Perhaps she also thought a change of clothing would help her avoid her attacker.

"Is that it?" asked Chib.

Brenda nodded. "That's all we have of her coming in. There are only a few cameras inside. Patient confidentiality. I'll forward to catch her coming out." She fast-forwarded the footage. She caught Garrick glancing at the time on his phone. "Don't worry, love, I know roughly when that is."

Garrick quickly put his phone away. "No, I wasn't... I have a funeral I have to go to."

Brenda leaned over and took a thin plastic folder from her in tray, and handed it to Chib. "Her checking-in records."

Chib read the printout through the clear plastic folder. "Galina al-Dulaimi. She was twenty."

Garrick took the offered page. There were scant details, and an address he was sure was false. "What was she doing here?"

"Her appointment was with the osteopath, but beyond that, I can't tell you no more. You'll have to make an official request for her records." She flashed him a smile. "I didn't make the rules, love, or I'd give it to you in a heartbeat."

Garrick couldn't help but smile. She was definitely flirting with him. Chib gave a little uncomfortable cough; she was sitting between them.

Brenda pointed to the screen. "But I can tell you she was in and out in fifty minutes. So..." she slowed the footage down. "She should be coming..." she teased her sentence out. "Right about... now!"

Galina was leaving in a hurry while typing on her phone. She headed straight out of the door.

"Hold on a tick," Brenda said as she swapped video cassettes and forwarded to the same time code.

They watched Galina exit, but she didn't head back the same way she'd arrived. Instead, she stopped and looked around. Then she must have seen somebody, as she hurried across the car park and out of the camera's field of view.

"Can we see who she's meeting?"

Brenda was already looking through a plastic box containing more tapes. She selected one and loaded it up. Nobody spoke as another camera view, from a pole in the car park, appeared on the screen. In moments she found the correct time code, and they watched Galina cut diagonally across the lot, heading towards the exit.

There was a black Audi parked just beyond the entrance gate. It was too far for the camera to make out the registration, but Garrick recognised the model. An Audi A1. The same model and colour as Peter Thorpe's impounded car.

A man climbed from the passenger seat and opened the rear door, hurrying her inside. Again, he was too far for the camera to pick up a detailed image, but from his heavy set and balding head, Garrick would gamble his scant life savings that it was Mircea.

A snort of recognition from Chib confirmed his hunch.

"We've got him, Chib. We've got the bastard."

21

Although it wasn't far, Garrick was pushing the speed limit as he drove down the M20 to Folkestone. There had been no more snow, and the gritters had done a sterling job preparing the motorway, but it was still far from ideal driving conditions.

Turning off, the roads became treacherous again as he hurried towards Hawkinge Cemetery. Chib had returned to the station to formally charge the Romanian trucker, just in the nick of time, before they had to release him. Garrick wished he could have done so, just to see the arrogant smile fall from his face. But he couldn't risk missing the chance to meet Manfri at his father's funeral. He was critical in sewing up Jamal's connection with Mircea.

Meeting at the funeral was less than desirable for another reason, other than Manfri's own grief. The last time Garrick had been to one was two months ago, for Sam McKinzie's, the man he had thought would be his brother-in-law, before he'd been found hacked apart on a ranch in Illinois. It had taken a while for the body to be repatriated, so the funeral had taken place a week before Christmas in Berkshire, close to the house they had just bought.

He recalled little about the day, other than the endless parade of people telling him how sorry they were for his loss. And it wasn't even his sister's funeral. Whether she would ever have the dignity of one, he couldn't say, but being at somebody else's brought that nagging concern back.

DC Sean Wilkes had seen reports that the town's inhabitants were not happy with having a Traveller funeral procession through their streets, let alone one of them buried in the local graveyard. It reminded Garrick of the intolerance he'd seen reflect in Stan's eyes back in Wye. Duke might be laid to rest in an unmarked pauper's grave, but the locals felt it would leave a stain on the town. The Travellers had settled on the southwest side of Hawkinge; the graveyard was to the north, so they had little choice but to cut straight through.

Garrick drove up Spitfire Lane to the roundabout and was mid-turn onto Aerodrome Road when he slammed on the brakes. His Land Rover's arthritic engine coughed and stalled. He stepped out of the car for a better look. Ahead, the road was blocked by a wall of people. It wasn't just Kezia's community. Large numbers from other travelling communities had come to pay their respects to Duke, or at least to ensure he stayed buried.

Leading the procession were six people in white shirts and ties, playing fiddles and trumpets in a lively, if slightly discordant, tune. Two horses came next, with splendid feathers on their heads, snorting great puffs of steam into the frigid air. They pulled a cart draped with flowers and colourful ribbons woven around Duke's casket.

Four more horse-drawn wagons followed. A grim-faced Kezia sat with the driver of the lead wagon, and next to her a man in his twenties, with wild, unkempt hair and stubble on his chin. He had smouldering dark eyes and, in another world, movie-star looks. Garrick was certain this was Manfri. He looked sidelong at the smattering of locals who lined the street. Some returned his hostile look, others holding children, were merely fascinated by the spectacle.

Behind the wagons, more Romani walked next to trucks and cars that had been garishly decorated with colourful ribbons. They all beeped their horns. Every mourner wore something white, and there was the occasional splash of red too. The emotion worn on their faces was tangible, brows heavily furrowed, and some were openly weeping.

The procession stretched as far as Garrick could see. He estimated there were over three-hundred people in all. Kezia caught his eye as the procession turned into the cemetery road. It took several minutes for the last of the group to pass by. Garrick parked his vehicle up on the kerb and followed them inside.

He waited outside the church, which stood at the centre of the cemetery. It was just as well because the mourners spilled from the doorway, such were their numbers. He kept glancing at his phone to read updates from Chib about Mircea's foul-mouthed response to being formally arrested. Apparently, his English had improved dramatically.

Then the funeral procession emerged from the church. Six grim-faced men carried Duke's casket, with Manfri positioned on a leading corner. Kezia led the mourners, who clung to one another in a rising tide of emotion. Garrick was struck at how composed Kezia was.

As they lowered the coffin into the open-grave, Garrick noticed a familiar face at the edge of the crowd. Curious, he stepped closer.

"Trisha?"

Trisha Warren didn't immediately recognise him, but when she did, she looked more shocked than surprised.

"Detective Garrick."

She was wearing a black suit, a white shirt under her jacket, and sensible wellies.

"I'm surprised to see you here."

"I helped arrange the funeral with the local priest. It's times like these when the church is needed to stitch communities together."

"It looks as if you have done a fine job."

She took the compliment with a silent nod and remained fixed on the activity at the grave.

"Do you work at lot with this community?"

"There's always work to be done when society doesn't accept you. And how is your investigation going with the girl?"

"Making waves," he replied cryptically. It seemed enough of a response for her.

"Tell me, do you think these folks get used as much as the refugees?"

"Used? You mean exploited?" She nodded. "They get bad mouthed, and painted as the aggressors, then they get used and exploited by the real criminals."

"Such as?"

"It's not for me to say, detective."

"If you want me to be more succinct, then how about drugs? Particularly ones ferried through this community."

He watched as Trisha tensed and didn't immediately reply. When she did, she picked her words with care.

"Drug use is not a particular problem with them, or the

refugees. That tends to be a working class burden. These people are considered below that."

"I didn't say *use*, I said ferried. Passing through the community in a classic county lines operation. I know it's happening."

"Was," Trisha quickly interjected. She wrestled with how much to say. "It began and ended with Duke. He used the community to sell to local dealers. He'd been involved in many a scam in the past, believe me, but this was the easiest money maker he'd ever made."

They watched as mourners tossed wreathes into the grave. Kezia didn't. Her eyes never left the casket, as if worried in doing so, the occupant might escape.

"Kezia had wanted it stopped. As did most of the others. They knew it would bring nothing but ill-fortune down on them. And they were right."

Alarm bells were ringing in Garrick's mind. She had given no hint that she knew Jamal or Galina. He studied Trisha carefully, but she seemed oblivious to his interest. "It sounds like you worked closely with them?"

She shook her head. "Only Kezia, really. She came to the church, and that's where I heard about their problems. They need money to live, so where are they supposed to get it? They don't qualify for government benefits, and nobody is exactly in a rush to employ them."

"So crime is the only way."

She gave a humourless laugh. "That is the easy way out, detective. I told you Guiding Hands has been working to help them find legal employment. Refugees, Travellers, anybody who needs it. I have had a lot of success finding them work on farms around here. It's not pleasant work. It's backbreaking and the hours are long, but it pays. Gives them the hope of a normal life."

When Garrick looked back, the funeral was dispersing. He saw Kezia standing aside, talking to Manfri. His head was bowed, but he kept casting looks towards Garrick. They were evidently talking about him, and just as obvious was his reluctance to engage with the police. The matriarch won out, and they both began walking towards him.

"How well did you know Jamal?"

"Who?"

Did she pause fractionally before replying? Or had she simply not been paying attention? Her face gave nothing away as she gave a terse smile and a little wave to Kezia as they joined them.

"Thank you for arranging this," Kezia said to her in a low voice.

"Of course. If there is anything more I can do, then call me. You have my number." She nodded to Garrick. "Detective" Then she walked towards the church, never once looking at Manfri.

Up close, Manfri was even better looking that Garrick had thought, and wondered what it would take to turn Trisha's head.

"She said you're investigating Jay's murder," he said, almost in a low growl. Both hands kept nervously balling into fists. Whether from talking to the police or the weight of having to bury his father, it was impossible to tell.

"Did Jamal have a last name?"

"Not one I asked. No need. She was leaving her past behind and didn't need to drag it with her. Have you found him?"

It was a pointed question.

"We have a suspect in custody."

"It was that bloody Mircea, wasn't it? I should've killed him meself."

Kezia barked at him in rapid Romani. He snapped in reply, but hung his head solemnly.

"He didn't mean that, sir," Kezia said. "It's all the emotion of the day."

Garrick nodded in understanding. "I can quite believe that. I wouldn't worry. I didn't hear him say a thing."

He caught Manfri's look and hoped that he'd earned a modicum of trust. No, he hadn't; it was just a flicker of curiosity.

"I need to know everything about Mircea." He saw a wall of reluctance raise. "This is not about grassing him up, or any misguided code of honour. This is purely about establishing Jamal's life and making sure whoever killed her, pays for it."

Manfri rolled on the balls of his feet. He swapped a look with Kezia, who gave the smallest nod of approval.

"Okay, then. I'll tell ya. But it will cost ya a drink."

22

The barman at the Mayfly pub was probably a student, but the look he gave Manfri was poison. In his cheap suit and thin black tie, he was easily marked out as belonging to the funeral precession. The scattering of locals, hunched over their pints, were equally hostile.

"We don't serve your kind in here," the barman said quietly to Garrick.

Garrick leaned in and dropped his voice. "Sorry, I had trouble hearing you, lad. Which is just as well, as discrimination is illegal." He slowly held up his police ID card until it was in the boy's face.

The barman paled and set about pouring a Guinness and half a pint of lager. Garrick pointed to the Guinness.

"And it's mighty good of you to offer him that on the house. He has just lost his father." He picked up the half. "I'll pay for this, of course."

Taking a table in the corner, Manfri took a long slow sip of Guinness and closed his eyes, savouring the taste.

"I thought you people didn't drink?"

"What? Gypsies?"

"Romani. In my, admittedly slim, research, I thought you practice Hindu beliefs as well as Catholic ones?"

"It's not forbidden. And it's not as if we're the Irish." He glanced at Garrick's half-pint. "I thought you people drink all the time?"

"What? Cops? You'd be right there. To your father." He raised the drink in salute. Manfri didn't reciprocate. "First off, I apologize for having to do this after your loss. I appreciate it."

Manfri shrugged. "Not many will miss him."

"Tell me about Mircea."

"What do you know?"

Garrick sighed. This wasn't a game he wanted to play, but there was nothing to be gained in alienating Manfri.

"That he found Jamal hiding in his lorry. Rather than turn her over to the authorities, he made her sell drugs. She didn't want to, but how could she say no? I know you found her and gave her shelter in your community."

"It was September last year. We were near Hythe. Me and two of the other lads were coming back from work when we found her. She'd been mugged. She was shaking, bleeding, frightened. And she still looked like an angel." His voice cracked and he sipped his drink.

"You were working?"

"You sound surprised? Do you think I was breaking into cars or robbing pensioners?" He looked defiantly at Garrick.

"You'll have to forgive me. I am not good at hiding my ignorance."

"The church organises work. I saw you speaking with Trisha. She's one of the few good ones." He looked reflective.

"It was a job picking vegetables on a farm. Paid bugger all and was backbreaking. I hated it. But had I not taken that job, I would never have met Jay." He sighed and propped his elbows on the table, running both hands through his hair. "She had nowhere to stay, so I took her in. I tried nothing on, before you ask."

"I wasn't going to. It's very clear you were in love."

He nodded. "Only *tata* didn't see it that way. He wanted her out. Thought she was a whore. Just another *gadji*. That was until he found out about the drugs." He collected his thoughts. "She wasn't selling much, so don't judge her. She hated it. I'd offered to get some of the lads to sort Mircea out, but she was against that, too. She worried he'd take it out on the others he had doing his dirty work. And now me Tata had her between a rock and a hard place. He was happy to take them off her hands and wanted more. He could see how we could get it wider. In the farms, in the towns, and he'd reap the profits. I wouldn't do it, but Jay felt the pressure. Thought she was responsible for driving me and Duke apart. Truth was, we always hated one another. This just reinforced it."

"So, she took more drugs from Mircea?"

"That's about it. She threatened to stop, and Duke threatened to ban her from the community. She told the Romanian she'd pack it in, and he threatened to have her deported. What could she do?"

He fell into a thoughtful silence as he stared at the white head on his drink.

"So I suggested we leave together. I got more family out in the West Country. She was up for that, but she wanted to do more with her life. Typical, Jay." He smiled fondly. "She was unstoppable when she wanted to be. She decided to turn herself in and claim asylum. She wanted to stay here properly. Then she and I could do whatever we wanted."

"That was a brave decision."

"Aye. She talked it through with Trisha, who said she could organise everything."

Again, Garrick felt edgy. Trisha had offered none of this information. Details that would have helped him solve the case much earlier. What was she hiding?

Manfri continued. "Knowing what she'd decided, Duke insisted on meeting Mircea himself. He reckoned he didn't need her, not that she was keeping any of the money. He took every penny."

"I was told Mircea came to visit."

"He was a hated man. Nobody liked what Duke was doing, and him doing a deal with Mircea threatened to make it worse. Me and Jay just wanted to turn our backs on the whole sorry mess and go."

"The night before she died, she went to see Mircea. Why? If she had already told him she was going to turn herself in, what was left to discuss?"

Manfri smiled sadly. "Ah, that would be greed, detective. Y'see, me tata knew he had a valuable supply line. Jay didn't care about such things, but he knew the value, so knew that Mircea could be screwed for a bigger cut of the profits. That's what they argued about when Mircea came."

Garrick had assumed it had been Mircea and Jamal arguing. Kezia hadn't been clear.

"Maybe Mircea saw this as a coup, I dunno. But it was obvious he would not let that happen. He weren't going to let Duke screw him over. And the only other link he had to the community was..."

"Jamal."

"He needed her and had no grip on her. So he set her up. She got a call asking to meet. All friendly, no hard feelings, like. He was even offering a new cut of coke. Better quality, I don't know. He wanted her to pass it on to Duke as a token they needed to talk. Renegotiate."

Manfri was becoming restless. He leaned back in his chair and took in the pub. The other customers had given up casting disapproving looks and were now quietly talking and laughing. Business as usual.

"She met him in his lorry."

"Aye. When she got there, he weren't there. She waited. He didn't show. There was a message in the truck telling her to meet him on the hill. He wanted to try to talk her out of it, or wish her good luck if he couldn't. Stupidly, she felt some sort of loyalty. He had been the one to bring her over and hadn't turned her in, true to his word. She went to talk to the other bloke who works with him. He had the samples to pass on to Duke. She called me. I picked her up and took her to Castle Hill."

Everything was slotting neatly into Garrick's new world view.

Manfri was reluctant to continue. He kept glancing between his drink, Garrick, and the rest of the room.

"What happened on the hill is quite critical, Manfri. And you were there, weren't you?"

Manfri nodded. He took a long gulp of Guinness, putting the glass down harder than he intended.

"It didn't make sense to me why he would want to meet there, and not in his truck, like they arranged. I was safer for him there. It felt all wrong. I know why now, of course. He was going to kill me tata."

Garrick's drink froze halfway to his lips. He slowly lowered the glass as he absorbed that revelation.

"Mircea wanted to kill Duke? Wouldn't that completely ruin his network?"

"It was ruined, anyway. This might solve it. Kill him and lay the blame at Jay's feet. What do you think a murder charge would do to her asylum application? You don't know what it's like to be exploited. What it's like to have nothing to lose. Who do you turn to? The law? Friends? Family?"

If there was a knighthood for being a grade-A bastard, then it sounded as if Mircea would be the perfect recipient. Garrick really couldn't blame Manfri for wanting him dead.

"So, what happened on the hill?"

23

J amal shivered as she climbed out of Manfri's car. The heater in the battered Golf had stopped working long ago, but it was still warmer than the constant wind.

"You shouldn't be doing this," Manfri said as he hurried to follow her.

It was drizzling, but the wind chilled them both. Manfri had parked the car on Crete Road, close to the metal posts that prevented vehicular access on to the hill. Jamal adjusted the two kilo plastic wrapped bags she had stuffed in her jacket's inside pockets. She hated that Peter Thorpe had asked her to do this, but consoled herself that it was the final time. With frozen fingers, she switched her mobile's torch on and illuminated the narrow path that cut around the hill. It was soft with mud from days of rain, but it could have been worse. Manfri followed closely behind, muttering with every step.

Taking it in turns to pass through a wooden kissing gate, Jamal tried to reassure Manfri that this was for the best. From tomorrow, she could start her life out of the shadows. She didn't share his concern that they may send her back to Iraq.

The nice woman at Guiding Hands had assured her that her case was a strong one, bolstered because Christians there were being persecuted at the hands of other groups.

They passed under sagging power cables strung from a tower and heard the gentle hiss as rain pelted them. The trail became steeper, and she smiled when she heard Manfri panting for breath. Most of her journey from Iraq had been on foot, so a tiny hill like this posed no problem. Ahead, the curve of the hill offered tantalising glimpses of the yellow and white streetlights of Folkestone far below.

The path clung to the edge of the hill, and more lights from the town became visible, including a constant line of headlights moving back and forth across the M20.

"I will go to university and study law," she declared. She had told Manfri about her plans many times, but she enjoyed talking aloud about her dreams. It was a superstition, but she believed that only by speaking about them could they come true. It had worked during the arduous crossing to the UK. "I will help others like me. I will make sure the Romani have true freedom." In the darkness, she punched the air and smiled. "I will make life great for us all!"

She turned to check he was okay – her torch blinding him.

"Jay!" he hissed, covering his eyes. His night vision was shot. "Now I can't see a thing!"

"There is nothing to see. Just me!" she said, pressing on.

"And that is the best thing to see," he said, blindly groping for her. She giggled and quickened her pace, keeping just out of reach.

The trail plateaued as they reached the top of the hill. A concrete cylinder had been placed there to signal the summit. From here they could look down at the lights of

Folkestone International, with trains berthed against the platforms, ready to venture into the Tunnel and across to France. To the left of that was a spangled vista of lights defining Folkestone before they stopped in the distant darkness of the English Channel.

"It's beautiful up here," she said, taking in the view.

Manfri sat on the cylinder to catch his breath and considered that it was the first time anybody had referred to Folkestone as 'beautiful.' It was certainly quiet. Other than the patter of rain and gusting wind, there was nothing.

"Are you sure you got the time right?"

She checked her phone. It was approaching twelve-thirty. "He'll be here."

"Jay, please, let's go. He knows where we'll be. Let him come to us."

There was a sudden movement in the darkness, followed by muffled swearing. Manfri stood, positioning himself protectively between Jamal and the stranger. Jamal raised her phone's torch–

Casting light over Duke. He raised his hand over his eyes to stop himself from being blinded.

"Jesus Christ, girl! Point it away!"

His voice was slurred, and she could smell the familiar odour of alcohol even from here. Their caravan reeked of the stuff.

"Tata? What the hell are you doing here?"

"I got a message saying Mircea had something for me to celebrate our new partnership."

"I thought that wasn't happening?" Manfri and Jamal exchanged a confused look.

"Must've had a change of heart."

Jamal reached into her coat and produced the two bags of

cocaine. "I suppose he means these. I was told to give them to you." She threw them deliberately short. Duke scrambled in the damp grass towards them.

"Careful, you stupid cow!"

"They said it was worth twice as much." She held up her hands to disown it. "Take it. It is yours now. I am having nothing more to do with this."

Duke knelt to retrieve them, his arthritic knees clicking. He hugged the packets close to his chest like they were his children.

"Then I don't have any need for you. You'll have to find somewhere else to lay your head."

"Tata–" Manfri said with a warning growl.

Duke tried to stand, but his knees wouldn't obey. "You can shut up! I give you a home, and you betray me by siding with *this*," he snarled disparagingly at Jamal.

Manfri wouldn't be pushed down. "We are going back, tata. The rest of the community doesn't want you there. You find somewhere else."

"I don't care what they want. Or you. They'll do as I say. So will you, lad."

"See the mess you have caused, Jamal?"

They all turned to locate the source of the new voice. A large figure kept in the darkness, but the accent was unmistakable.

"Mircea?" Jamal said, turning her light on him. He was just at the edge of the LED's range.

"I said I will meet you here," he pointed a finger at Duke, "because I wanted you to see this. This is where greed gets you."

Duke tried to stand again, but his knee let him down. "Mircea. I was just sending this whore packing." He indicated the two bags he was still cradling. "More of this, and you and I will go a long way!" He laughed, deaf to the menace in the Romanian's voice.

Mircea's eyes didn't leave Jamal and Manfri.

"He's trying to get rid of you both. You know what it's like to be forced from your home, don't you, Jamal? And now he's doing it to you again. I want you to stay." He indicated Manfri. "Look what you have now. You have made a home with this fine young man." He stepped closer, looking Manfri up and down. "And you are far more a leader than he ever could be. Why should things change?"

Jamal shook her head. "I don't care. I have told you, there is nothing you can do to me." She turned to Manfri, casting the light on him. "Let's leave them to it."

Duke finally clambered to his feet. In the darkness, he didn't see Mircea's sudden burst of speed, but he felt the white-hot pain in his side. He gurgled in agony. Alerted, Jamal swung the light back around. Duke was clutching his stomach. It was difficult to see any detail in the darkness, or against his black coat, but the light caught the glint of a knife in Mircea's blood-soaked hand.

"Tata!" Manfri bellowed.

On autopilot, Jamal took a step forward and then stopped in shock. Manfri ran forward and caught Duke, but his weight brought both men down.

"What are you doing?" Jamal screamed. Her numb fingers tried to dial 112.

Mircea shield his eyes as Jamal's light blinded him. He lashed out, knocking the phone from her hand and striking her across the cheek. She fell onto her backside as the Romanian staggered over her in the darkness. She saw the blade in his hand.

Years of finely honed self-preservation reared inside her – and she ran. Glancing only behind, unable to see Manfri pinned by his father, but only hearing his voice in the distance.

"Jay! Jay! Where are you?"

24

DCI David Garrick supported himself on the bonnet of his jeep as the world around him swam unsteadily. The pain behind his eye throbbed again, and he swore he could hear the growth in his head as it tried to gnaw its way out.

Purely his imagination, he assured himself. He closed his eyes to let the wave of dizziness pass. In this state, he could barely walk, never mind drive.

With some gentle cajoling, Manfri had agreed to make a formal statement against the Romanian. He was less concerned with the death of his own father; he wanted to see Mircea hang from a tree for what he did to Jamal.

Cradling his bleeding tata, he had watched helplessly as both Jamal and Mircea disappeared down the side of the hill. By the time he followed, there was no sign of either of them. When he scrambled through the darkness and returned to Duke, he was weak and fading. Somehow, Manfri had got him to his car and returned to their caravan where Duke had died.

Of course, the police wouldn't be called. They never were. And with drugs in the mix, it could only come back to destroy their fragile community. Garrick couldn't believe he had been standing over Duke, standing over *another* victim of Mircea's, but with no idea how he had died.

The spinning abated. Garrick looked across the road to the cemetery. He didn't have the heart to tell Manfri that they would have to exhume his father straight after just laying him to rest. He wasn't sure how that factored into the Romani's view of death. That was a task he was more than happy to assign to Chib, especially as she had previously suggested such a thing.

He got behind the wheel and realised that the case was suddenly over.

No big crescendo. Just the gentle clatter of pieces falling together. He suddenly felt exhausted.

There were still several loose ends. The knife that killed Duke, and may have been used to carve up the girls, was missing. As was any hard evidence that placed the Romanian at the crime scene.

But they had a witness to one murder. Admittedly, a murder they didn't know about thirty minutes ago, but it would be churlish to complain. And they had video evidence that seemed to connect both Thorpe and Mircea to Galina on the morning of her death.

He called Chib to update her. She couldn't keep the delight out of her voice, and her cheer echoed from his hands-free speakers.

"I confronted Thorpe about him and Mircea picking Galina up at the hospital. He denied ever meeting her. Said he'd never been there."

"Do you blame him? It's another nail in his cell door. As I

recall, there was a dog walker who found Galina last year. Get Harry to ask her about the Audi. It may ring a few bells. Wait, better make it Wilkes instead, he's got a better manner than Harry. Oh, and good news. You get to exhume Duke's body."

"Me, sir?"

"It's going to take a truckload of paperwork to get permission. Right up your street, Chib."

"And where will you be, sir?"

"I'm heading to you now."

"Shouldn't somebody talk to Trisha Warren?"

"I was thinking about going down to the church to see her, but I decided against it."

"Why?"

"She hasn't exactly been forthcoming during any of our little chats, so I'm going to get uniform to pick her up. With any luck, it will rattle her enough to start talking."

Garrick's assessment on how Trisha Warren would react had been a colossal understatement. He had left her to stew in the interview room, while Harry circulated around the rest of the jubilant team and bullied them to come to his delayed birthday drinks, now set for tomorrow night as a combine birthday/victory celebration.

Carrying a folder of printed images, Garrick walked in on Trisha, who was in floods of tears. It took him a good five minutes and a cup of tea to calm her down. She sat, folded in her chair like a mouse, blowing her nose and stuttering for breath.

"Do I need a solicitor?"

"Only if you feel you should have one present. You are not being charged with anything, Miss Warren. But it appears you have been less than forthcoming when I have asked you questions."

She noisily blew her nose. "I have answered every question you have asked me."

Garrick pinched the bridge of his nose. The headache hadn't really gone away during the drive, and he was feeling irritable. He could already tell the type of person Trisha was. Somebody who thought they were smart and always a step ahead of the game. Just that she was a happy-clappy Christian who, admittedly, did plenty of good for others, didn't mean he had to indulge her.

"Tell me, Trisha, did you train in the legal profession?"

"Why yes. I studied for the LLB and then my diploma."

"But not the LDC?"

She pulled a face and primly sipped the tea from a paper cup. "I failed the LLB," she replied curtly. "It wasn't my type of thing, after all. I preferred to help out at the Citizen's Advice. Much more rewarding."

Garrick nodded. She failed the qualification to even *study* becoming a solicitor. That explained a great deal.

"I see. That explains why you only answer questions in a very *specific* way."

She opened her mouth to argue, but thought better of it.

"Where to begin? You claimed never to have seen Galina."

"I never said such a thing."

"I was with you at Napier when we showed everybody her picture." He took Galina's picture from the folder and slid it towards her. Trisha barely looked at him.

"You never actually asked me if I knew her. And no, I did not. To be honest, she was vaguely familiar, but they all do look the same, don't they?"

Garrick blinked in surprise at the veneer of racism. Trisha apparently didn't seem to beware of it as she continued.

"I see many waifs and strays, Detective. They come into

the church, they ask for our help. Unless we have to, we make a point of never taking details down. They see that as an authoritarian sign, and that's the last thing we want."

"You knew the Romani community quite well."

Trisha shrugged. "You never asked me about them."

"No, but I mentioned Jamal was connected to them." He took Jamal's picture out. A sadness crossed her face, and she gave an involuntary sob.

"I know what she looks like, Detective. I was trying to help the poor girl."

Garrick leaned forward, propping his elbows on the table. "And it never occurred to you that *I* may need to know every little detail? We have been working flat out trying to find her murderer. Every detail, no matter how irrelevant *you* think it is, could be important."

"She was here illegally. She came to me for help, and I helped. To be honest, when she told me she wanted to claim asylum, and her dreams about studying law, she reminded me of... me. But much smarter and more determined." She clutched her damp tissue against her breast. "I still have friends in the legal profession, so I really thought I could do something different with her."

She fidgeted in her seat. "To be honest, most of the people we try to help never really stand a chance. Many are denied a future here and sent back. Most don't have the skills to set up a new life. Do you know how high the suicide rate is amongst refugees? It's awful. With Jamal, I saw a real chance to make a difference. For *her* to make a difference."

"Walk me through that."

Trisha's eyes rolled to the ceiling. Garrick wasn't sure if she was trying to recall or editing her reply.

"She told me she was in trouble with the man who

brought her over here. That's not uncommon. I didn't pry, but I offered her some counselling for sexual abuse services. Which she didn't take." She said the last in a whisper, her cheeks flushing. Garrick realized that talking about murder was fine, but sex is where Trisha Warren drew the line. "I was not aware of the drugs issue until Manfri told me."

"You had known him before Jamal."

"Yes. He is a charmer." She blushed again. "Very bright, too. He came to some of our congregations and asked about *legal* paid work. One of our programmes places low-skilled workers in seasonal employment."

"You mean menial tasks nobody else wants to do?"

"Work that the more fortunate citizens of this country can't be bothered to do. It still needs doing. One of my successes is with the farming community. Tiring work, but honest. I put Manfri on one of those."

"He must have enjoyed that."

"He hated every second. But that's how he met Jamal." Her tale of how they met matched Manfri's own account. "He was the one who brought her to me for help. So, the first thing I did was to put her on a farming project. I hoped that if she was earning some money honestly, then she could break away from… whatever it was she was being forced to do."

"You never asked her? Even if you thought it was prostitution rather than drugs?"

"It is not my role to make judgement calls. I'm trying to help them. If I know of anything illegal… well, that's a terrible moral tangle, isn't it? She didn't want labouring work. I think Manfri had warned her off it. We had discussions about her legal status her. She had a terrific case for asylum."

"Did you know that Manfri's father was using her?"

"Only after his death. When Kezia asked for help to arrange the funeral."

"You did an amazingly quick turnaround on the arrangements."

"The Romani people don't like the dead to linger around too long."

"And that's when you were told about the drugs?" She nodded. "By which time you also knew Jamal had been murdered. You knew she was living with the Travellers. And you knew I was looking for evidence amongst the refugee camp. And still... you remained silent." He raised his hands in confusion. "Please, help me out here. I don't understand..." She was quickly becoming one of the most frustrating people he had ever dealt with.

"I think, perhaps it's a question of ethics."

"Now I'm fascinated. Please educate me."

"The poor girl dies–"

"Was *murdered*, that's a technical distinction," Garrick interjected sarcastically, then prompted for her to continue.

"And Manfri loses his father at the same time. Tell me, how humane is it to tell the police that the two deceased were involved in drugs. Particularly when one of them was doing so against her own will? You would descend on an already ravaged and maligned community for what reason?"

"Because the drugs were connected to both their deaths."

"That was not apparent to me."

"It doesn't matter whether it is apparent to you or not!" Garrick cried incredulously. "You withheld evidence!"

Trisha looked shocked, and a rapid bout of halting breaths prevented her from replying. Tears welled in her eyes, and Garrick couldn't help but wonder if they were crocodile ones. He was losing his temper. "Let me tell you the picture you're painting for me. Guiding Hands is more about your ego than it is about helping others."

"Not true!"

He steamrolled over her. "And you saw that if Jamal was successful in claiming asylum, getting her degree, then you suddenly have a poster child for your charity. All because of you!" Trisha's eyes narrowed in anger. "And the very reason you chose not to tell me you knew her is because the moment you discovered she was involved with drugs, it would come back and bring your whole charity down. All that good work you've been doing would be gone, like that." He slammed his palm on the desk, making her jump. "Your poster child was suddenly a liability! That's why you withheld evidence from me!"

"I withheld nothing, detective! You are accusing me of not answering questions you didn't ask!"

It took a moment for Garrick to untangle that sentence in his head. Then he laughed at her audacity when he realised that she'd twisted the accusation round to blame him. He paused the interview and had to leave the room to calm down.

After a couple of Ibuprofen swilled down with lukewarm green tea, he returned for more punishment. Trisha's hysterics appeared to have vanished during the break, too.

"Tell me about Galina." He tapped her picture as a reminder. It had not moved from where he'd originally set it in front of her. "And please, fill in the blanks of any question I so naively fail to ask."

"I have already told you everything. It was last year, I don't recall. I don't even think I knew her name. The only help she wanted was to find work."

"The farm labouring?"

"Yes. And she was good at it. I tell them where to go, and they go. It's that transparent. They know their employer has been vetted by Guiding Hands, so they're not going to be abused and will definitely be paid. And that's the only inter-action we have. They only come back if they need to complain, and that doesn't happen."

"Do you remember which farm she worked on?"

"One in Brabourne. We place a lot there. I don't know how long she stayed. As I say, we don't hear from the employees unless there is a problem, and the employers only contact me if they need more people, or have a complaint themselves."

"May I have the address?"

"Of course."

He handed her a pen from the folder and asked her to write it on the back of Galina's photograph.

"One last thing, and then I will get an officer to take you home." He took the final photo out. It was one of Mircea ushering Galina into the back of the Audi. "Have you ever seen this man before?"

She looked long and hard before finally answering. "I'm not sure."

"Take your time."

"It's not very good quality."

"Squint." He was joking, but she did so anyway.

"It does look a little like Mr Constantine. I'm guessing that's Galina. It's hard to tell."

Garrick propped his elbows on the table and steepled his fingers across his mouth. He had a sudden feeling that he was in for a longer night than he anticipated.

"Mr Constantine?"

Trisha pulled a face and nodded. "It would make sense if

it was. He's a businessman who is occasionally over from Bucharest. He helps us a lot in placing people who wish to work, right across Kent, East Sussex, and Surrey, in fact. Nice chap. He does a lot of work at Brabourne. Handles their import-exports, I believe."

Garrick didn't quite know what to say. Just how much should he reveal? His duty was to solve the murders, not the drugs network. That was the domain of the National Crimes Agency, and they already had a team waiting to sweep in. Perhaps he should go to Brabourne Farm with a member of that team. It could be a nice symbolic handing over of the baton just before he closed his own case.

25

Superintendent Margery Drury could not stay so aloof in the face of a job well done. She beamed her praise at the whole of Garrick's team. She even congratulated DC Harry Lord, who she normally preferred to keep at the end of a stern look.

"You should come and celebrate with us tonight, ma'am! This, and my birthday!"

Drury's smile widened. "Harry, I couldn't think of anything I'd rather do less!"

Harry expected nothing less. Drury never joined the proles in the pub, but she was canny enough to pre-pay a round or two in advance when she was in a good mood. And this morning, she was in a fantastic one. Solving the case was praiseworthy enough, but it seemed Mircea's enterprise was turning into a major county lines operation. One that meant his job as a truck driver was nothing more than a cover he used to run his real business.

Duke's body had been exhumed that very morning, in what she considered could be a record-breaking short burial.

Fanta confirmed that his cause of death would be known by lunchtime.

Garrick had started the day, for the first time in a while, with a sense of optimism and without the dull throb of a headache. There were more surprises in store with the arrival of a text message from Wendy. It was a vague: *are you doing anything this weekend?* But to Garrick it was as if a firework had jolted his senses. Perhaps the date hadn't been such a disaster after all? He resolved to focus some of his detective skills on his own love-life.

There were smiles throughout the incident room as Drury shook everybody's hand. Even the members of the team she was only vaguely aware existed, and assured them that their magnificent diligent work wouldn't go unnoticed. Garrick didn't have the heart to tell her that there were still a lot of holes in the case.

Then, at 10:36, he didn't have to. The report came in.

Another murder.

Another young girl.

Another skinning.

The jubilation in the incident room vanished in an instant. Drury rounded on Garrick and Chib, who looked more shocked than anybody else.

"*Another* murder," Drury echoed. "Then who the hell have we arrested?"

Garrick was thinking the same thing, but was savvy enough to keep his mouth shut. Chib, however, was too new to know when to stay silent.

"Maybe it's a copycat, ma'am. Maybe there's a third–"

"There is never room for 'maybe' on my team, DS Okon. Is that clear?" The ice in Drury's voice was cooler than the fresh snow outside.

Before any more of his team could be sacrificed to Drury's temper, Garrick broke the spell by sharply clapping his hands and barking orders.

"Wilkes, Lord, you're coming with me and Chib to the scene."

Fanta moved to intercept Garrick. "Can I come too? Please?" She cast a look at Drury, who was stomping from the incident room in a volcanic temper.

"I need you here."

Fanta rolled her eyes like a petulant teenager. Garrick was so wired that he almost snapped and pulled rank before stopping himself. DC Liu's attitude was a quirk he could live with, and her performance had been exceptional. He needed her onside.

He pointed at the evidence board. "Go through everything. I want bullet points of every hole and unknown we have." Fanta frowned. "For example, we know Mircea left his cab and met Jamal at Castle Hill, but we don't know how he got there." That point in particular had been nagging him. He had originally thought it had been Duke, but Manfri's confession had squashed that idea, and he'd had little time to give it any further thought. "And the skin. We need to know more about this trophy hunting behaviour." He saw the disappointment on her face. "Think of it as our special project."

"A dog walker?"

"Yes, sir," said the young constable, standing at the edge of the police tape. She was wearing a sensible padded all-weather jacket, a reminder that Garrick was, as usual, underdressed.

"Poor sods. It's always the dog walkers stumbling over something gruesome. I'd stick to a cat."

White Hill Road had been sealed from the Challock side where it joined Faversham Road, right down to where it ended at the A28. The road running along Kings Wood had a thin layer of snow on it. Several first responder police cars were parked to the side. Garrick's team had parked in the middle of the road to preserve any evidence in case the killer had parked on the verge. The poor dog walker had been ferried back to the station for their statement to be taken.

Garrick and Chib ducked under the police tape and cautiously approached the body that was bound to a tree just ten yards from the road. DC Wilkes and Lord stayed back, taking down details from the officers who had arrived first.

"Single file, Chib," said Garrick, as he carefully picked his way through the snow. He was making sure not to trample any prints, not that he could see any. They stopped within four feet of the body. The surrounding area showed signs of many footprints that had since been half-filled by fresh snow. The girl was completely naked, her blue dress and panties tossed casually aside. Her hands had been bound so tightly by cable ties that she was still upright against the tree. The snow around her feet was deep red, three feet in every direction. She had bled freely as the skin was carved, leaving a grizzly display of muscle from the nape of her neck to below her buttocks. She looked more like a perfect anatomical mannequin than a real human being. The freezing temperature had preserved the wound and applied a layer of glistening frost across it.

Garrick adjusted his angle so he could see her face, framed by long, wavy blonde hair. Her skin was alabaster, blue eyes wide in agony and now frozen, along with a river of tears down her cheeks.

"He's getting more adventurous and taken a bigger swathe

of skin. And look at the lines. Smoother, not so ragged. And that is in the dark and the cold."

Chib was looking at the floor. "He didn't try to disguise his footprints." Not only were some of them in the blood, there were so many that they could easily trace them walking back from the corpse, keeping parallel to the road.

"Serial killers can get overconfident when they think they're unstoppable," said Garrick sombrely. "That's usually when they make a mistake." The trail of both his and her footprints leading to this spot was very clear. It didn't feel like a mistake. It felt like a statement.

"Sir, do you see her ankles?"

Garrick knelt for a better look. Her bare feet were covered by red snow and had been splayed apart. If the killer was following the same modus operandi as the others, it wouldn't be for sexual reasons. Garrick suspected it was to anchor the girl in place as she was carved up. The flesh above her ankles was bloodied, raw, and frozen.

"Foxes," Garrick said. He pointed to sets of paw prints milling around her legs. "They saw the chance for a free meal and took a chunk out of her."

The squeal of brakes from the main road signalled the arrival of two large white vans. SOCO had arrived. He and Chib backtracked to the road and told the forensic team where they had walked. The area was suddenly a flurry of activity.

Garrick extracted himself from the others and spotted the line of footprints that led away from the body. They were so close to the road that he could easily track them. They led a hundred yards further down to the entrance of the car park. The footprints stepped from the trees and were lost in snow that at least two vehicles had churned. The dog walker's car was still here, and doggers widely used the area.

He couldn't help feeling that the timing and nature of this murder was not random. As if they were being mocked for arresting the wrong people. That was nonsense, of course. He wasn't the target of anything; he was merely feeling frustrated. He went back to join the others. Standing around in the cold watching the SOCO team was also making him feel redundant. He nudged Chib's elbow and indicated his car.

"Let's go."

"Where?"

"We need to tick a few more boxes."

"Shouldn't we supervise this?"

Garrick waved his hand dismissively. "Let Harry and Wilkes do that."

He recognised the disappointment on Chib's face. During his stint as a DS, learning the ropes, there was always a frisson of excitement when SOCO arrived. It was only through experience that he acknowledged their job was slow and laborious. She'd soon learn that the glamour would wear off.

Brabourne Farm was only nine miles away, but across the treacherous snowy Downs it took close to forty-five minutes. His head throbbed from concentrating as he gripped the wheel tightly. The previous night's snowfall had only added a veneer to the previously cleared B-Roads, but when that had iced up, it led to moments of Chib gasping and clutching at the dash as the Land Rover's wheels occasionally slipped. Garrick had been in no danger of losing control, but he was relieved when they passed the welcoming whitewashed walls of the Five Bells pub in Brabourne. He turned at the old classic red phone box that reached from the snow like a bloody finger, beckoning them to their destination.

They had passed through Wye along the way, and Garrick resisted the urge to stop at the *Pilgrim's Tale Bookshop* to unload his new problems on John. His focus on the investigation had been off since returning from compassionate leave. Perhaps others would be more forgiving as they considered his circumstances. Garrick couldn't shake the feeling it had cost another life.

The connections between Guiding Hands and Brabourne were too strong to ignore. Two minutes later, they were at the end of the tract to Brabourne Farm. The recently laid black tarmacadam led to the main nest of buildings fifty yards from the road. They had cleared that very morning, and judging by the mounds of snow ploughed to the sides, it had been diligently cleared every day over the weekend.

They pulled into a three-sided courtyard, with a grand, red-bricked farmhouse to one side. The gable end was green with ivy reaching from the ground. Double glazing, a satellite dish and fresh pointing, showed that care and love had been lavished on it recently. Perpendicular to the house were four stables, the old doors replaced with sliding black shutters. A pair of plain white transit vans had been reversed into two of the open doorways. The other two were shut. The yard's third side was a huge barn. From the scaffolding and snow-laden plastic sheeting, major restoration work was underway.

Garrick and Chib stepped out from the car and were immediately struck by how cold the courtyard was, as if it possessed its own microclimate. A young Middle Eastern man was doing an admirable job of shovelling the snow into a wheelbarrow. He looked up with a simple nod. A scarf was wrapped around his head, and his puffer jacket had seen better days. They could see holes in his gloves, and Garrick suspected the only real thing keeping him warm was the effort he put into work.

"We should make a note of what they're paying these fellows," he said quietly to Chib. "I bet it's not minimum wage."

They approached the farmhouse and heard dogs yapping inside. There was a flagpole on the stable roof. As they approached, it hadn't been clear what it was, but from this angle they could tell it was a damp, limp Cross of Saint George. Garrick flicked a look at the young man who had resumed his snow clearing duties.

"That's going to make him feel welcome," he muttered.

He looked sidelong at the stables. Through the gaps between the vans and door, he could see people moving. Two of them were young women carrying boxes. He stopped to look at the vans. It took Chib a moment to register what he'd seen.

"Romanian plates."

Garrick nodded. "Make a note of them."

Chib used her phone to photograph the vehicles.

"What do you think you're doing?" snapped a voice from the farmhouse.

Garrick reached into his pocket for his ID card – then froze. He recognised the tall, thin, balding man glaring at him as he strode from the farmhouse. A pair of Alsatians ran out, no longer barking, but circling around Garrick and Chib, tails raised and sniffing inquisitively.

"Mr Fielding?" asked Garrick, recalling the farmer's name from the background info Fanta had emailed him? "Mr Stan Fielding?"

Stan evidently didn't recognise Garrick, but he could

perfectly recall the bitterness on the man's face as he sat in the café in Wye. He was wearing the same green wax jacket as he made a beeline straight for Chib, whose phone was still pointed at the vans.

Garrick sidestepped, blocking him and raising his ID card.

"DCI Garrick, this is DS Okon. We'd like to ask you a few questions."

Stan stopped in his tracks as if he'd struck an invisible wall. He said nothing. Garrick reached down and scratched between the ears of the dog that was sniffing at his coat. The Alsatian's tail wagged furiously; he was obviously a creature with more bark than bite.

"You're part of Trisha Warren's Guiding Hands programme?"

Stan visibly relaxed and nodded towards the snow-clearer. "I take a few of them. I find them useful to have around."

"I imagine there is not too much work to do this time of year. I believe you don't have livestock. So, what do you grow in the winter?"

Stan laughed, further relaxing. "Farms don't stop just because the weather turns. If anything, it's busier now as we try to get things repaired and ready for spring." He pointed to the barn. "There's always tons to be done."

"And I see you're exporting to Europe." He nodded at the vans.

"Wine. A bit of Kent sparkle to give them a run for their money."

"Very entrepreneurial."

Chib strolled towards the stables. Stan eyed her nervously but said nothing.

"Do you sell wholesale or direct?"

"Direct. Best way to make a profit is to control the market. What do the police want to know about my wine for? I have all the necessary licenses and export papers."

"Merely curious." Garrick unlocked his phone, noticing that there was no signal on the farm. He located the picture of Mircea ushering Galina into the car. "Does he look familiar?"

Stan stared long and hard. So long that Garrick was prompted to ask again.

"Mr Constantine. He's a business associate. Works with the church helping this lot." He nodded to the young man, who was now pushing the full wheelbarrow from the courtyard. "And he buys plenty of my wine."

"And the girl?"

"I really can't tell."

Garrick flicked through the pictures until he found the clear one of Galina.

"Her?"

There was no disguising Stan's reaction this time. He paled and stuttered before composing himself. "She worked here for a bit. Hard worker. Likeable. Gal, that was her name. Like that Wonder Woman actress. Looked a bit like her, too. She suddenly upped and left. Didn't even say goodbye. Those camel jockeys are all the same. I thought she might have got deported." He shrugged. "Happens a lot. They just vanish off the radar."

Garrick's gaze hardened. He hadn't liked Stan when John Howard had introduced him, and now his opinion had crystallised. Here was a man making a pretence of charitably helping those in need, when it was just a smokescreen to mine a vile seam of exploitation, using those too innocent and vulnerable to object as he lined his own pockets. Even if it wasn't physical murder, it was murder of the soul.

The clatter of a stable door opening made Stan jolt. He was clearly tense over something. Chib had opened one of the doors. Behind it was parked a gleaming black Audi A1.

Just like the one in the picture.

It wasn't Peter Thorpe's car, after all.

"Mr Fairfield, I would like to continue asking you questions down at the station, if you don't mind."

Garrick's tone made it clear that it wasn't a request.

26

This time she had been missed.

A worried boyfriend had made a report that very morning, panicking when his girlfriend hadn't returned home. Her description matched the girl they had found in Kings Wood, and Fanta was able to gather a lot of information quickly.

Sihana was Albanian and had been in the clutches of sex traffickers since she was fourteen, an all-too common occurrence there. She was considered exceptionally beautiful and transferred to the UK in the backseat of a car. On the surface, she was just another student coming to study. The reality was, escorting their victims on a ferry was the easiest way for the traffickers to get their premium rated girls in and out. In England, she would fetch a high price. Now barely eighteen, and her future was already over.

That was until she had rebelled and slipped from the clutches of her captors.

Sihana had then met her boyfriend, who was a volunteer at one shelter, and they had recently moved in together. She had care and attention lavished on her that she'd never experienced before. Her claim for asylum had been made, and it looked as if it would be a mere formality to be approved. All indications were that her life was starting anew.

Garrick's team worked under an oppressive, grim silence. The light-hearted gallows humour that was essential to survive such stressful circumstances had disappeared. Nobody spoke about it, but they all felt responsible for her death. A photo of her and her boyfriend hung on the evidence wall. They looked the perfect young couple, and that had just added to the sombre atmosphere.

Fanta had retreated to the bathroom for a quiet sob and returned to her desk in gloomy silence. Garrick noticed DC Wilkes squeeze her hand as he passed, but turned a blind eye. Fanta was desperately searching for any links between Sihana, Peter Thorpe, Stan Fielding, and Mircea. There was none she could find. Sihana had never been part of Trisha Warren's Guiding Hands programme.

Stan Feilding was being interviewed, but with no formal charges, they couldn't search the farm just yet. Fanta's hunch was that they wouldn't find any connections there, either.

She unloaded her lack of results to Garrick, who looked distracted most of the time.

"Did you hear me?" she prompted?

Garrick had zoned out. "Sorry. You said you thought we wouldn't find anything at the farm."

"After that. About where she was working. She got the job on her own merits. Nobody set it up for her."

Garrick nodded, but he wasn't really listening. On the drive back to the station, his phone had chimed with a voice-mail that had been left when he had no reception at the farm.

It was his consultant who had seen the results of the MRI and wanted him to come in to discuss. Today, preferably.

The implied sense of urgency was worrying.

"Or should I be telling all this to DS Okon?"

"Mmm?"

Ordinarily, DC Liu would snap something sarcastic and witty. Instead, she just sighed, deflated. "She was a waitress in a café. She got the job on her own merits. Her boyfriend was very proud. We should send somebody to check it out. Like me," she added hopefully.

Garrick nodded. He was too unfocused for such things. He'd left Chib to conduct Stan Feilding's interview, fishing for the merest of connections to Sihana. Galina had worked for him. Jamal was linked through the Romanian. It was all too much to be coincidence. A single link to the new victim would put Stan Fielding firmly at the centre of the investigation.

But such evidence was like finding hen's teeth.

"Okay, you go and find out as much as you can."

Fanta leapt to her feet, suddenly smiling. She had been desperate to be part of the frontline investigation from the beginning.

"Will do, sir!" The formal moniker was a sign of just how happy she was.

She snatched her coat from the back of her chair as Garrick walked to the evidence board to look at the map pinned there. They had added a fresh pin to Kings Wood.

"Where did she live?"

"Kennington."

He traced his finger along the map. It was just at the bottom of the hill where she was found.

"And this café?"

"Wye."

Garrick spun on his heels. "What is it called?"

Fanta laughed as she pulled her coat on. "You'll like this: *Wye Have Coffee?*"

DC Fanta Liu had been fuming as she took off her coat and sat back at her computer, mumbling about being a slave to HOLMES. Garrick had lavished praise on her for that vital titbit, and then told her he was going to the café instead. Her value lay in staying at the heart of things, and he wanted her to push the SOCO team for their initial findings.

Garrick drove too fast to Wye and triggered one of the M20 speed cameras that double flashed in his mirror to prove that he'd been nicked. He had been leaving a second message on his consultant's voicemail to arrange an appointment and had given up by the time he parked outside the café.

The owner, Margaret, had broken down in tears when she heard the news, and Garrick made her a cup of tea as she slumped at a corner table. She had been incredibly fond of Sihana. She was never on time because of the transport difficulties in getting to work, but she always stayed longer and never complained. She had been due in this lunchtime, and Margaret had put it down to her poor timekeeping.

Margaret wasn't much use when it came to talking about her customers. She had taken over on January third and was only just starting to recognise the regulars. She knew John Howard, of course. His bookshop was on the same block, and he was a creature of habit when it came to his cream teas. Sihana had commented on him too, as he never tipped. Not even a penny, which was unusual because the pretty Albanian could charm hefty tips from the most hardened customers. All of which she was allowed to keep, Margaret hastily added.

"What about him?"

Garrick showed her a picture of Stan Feilding he had taken in the station.

"Oh, yes. He's often in here, and I think quite smitten with her. A big tipper." That didn't fit the profile of the man Garrick met. John was renowned for his parsimonious attitude, and he had pegged Stan to be the same. The nationalist attitude, exploitation, Saint George's flag, he was far from a textbook example of somebody who would tip a foreigner. From what he had been told, Sihana's English was functional and heavily accented. The antithesis of what he assumed Stan tolerated. Unless, of course, he was trying to charm her into a false sense of security…

But he had now made a connection between Sihana and Stan Fielding. Unfortunately, Margaret had no security cameras, but Garrick was assured that there would be easily enough eyewitness corroboration. In fact, he made a note to pop in and confirm with John Howard before he left.

The picture of Peter Thorpe went unrecognised, but another of Mircea provoked a reaction. She was pretty sure that the Romanian had met with Stan here just last week.

Garrick hurried from the café, his mind whirling. He was halfway down the street to John's bookshop when he received a call from Fanta.

"Must be nice outside in the crisp, fresh air," she muttered. "I think I might be coming down with the lurgy in this stuffy office."

Garrick sighed wearily, but her sarcasm was a sign she had promising news to impart. He told her they now had a direct link between Fielding and Sihana. He needed Chib to keep him there and start the ball rolling so that they could search the farm.

Fanta filled him in on the forensic investigation. The girl was alive as the killer carved the skin from her back. She'd been left to bleed to death, but it was a toss-up whether exposure got to her first. Like the other victims, there was no sign of sexual abuse. The light dress and lack of footwear suggested she had met her attacker elsewhere, and a preliminary search of the car park suggested that she maybe had been marched from there, deeper into the forest.

In the snow, there were hints of a struggle and a chase, but it hadn't lasted long. Her execution had been slow and deliberate.

Garrick sensed she was holding something back, and indeed she was. Her last flourish came with a loud '*Ta-da!*'

"They found the knife that killed her. It was in the car park."

That was sloppy, considering the unhurried nature of her death.

Fanta continued. "The lab needs more time to confirm, but striations on the wounds and blade match!"

That was a breakthrough. Microscopic notches and imperfections on the blade would create the same patterns on the skin, which was firm evidence that the same murder weapon was used in all three incidents. And that usually meant the same killer wielded it. In this case, somebody who was perfecting his art of skin grafting.

"And they match the wound on Duke, too!"

Garrick looked up and down the street, as if searching for inspiration. "That is a problem. We know Mircea stabbed Duke. Manfri is willing to testify to it. He could have killed the first two girls, but since he's banged up, how did the same knife end up at Sihana's crime scene?"

"I think something else may thrill you. *I* found out," she

quickly amended. "Fielding's Audi is probably the one that picked up Galina at the hospital, but we can't be sure. But our Romanian friend was definitely the passenger..."

"Which indicates that Fielding was driving."

"Correct. So I checked with ANPR and guess what, it was also at the Orbital Park's McDonald's at the same time Jamal was waiting at the roundabout for Manfri to pick her up!"

"Feilding and Mircea were watching her. They followed them to Castle Hill."

"That fits with your idea that he was picked up at the back of the Truckstop."

Stan Feilding hadn't been just acting as the Romanian's business partner; he'd been taxiing him around so that he didn't have to use the lorry.

"The knife wasn't found because Mircea left it in the car. It was Stan's knife all along. That's how he was able to use it on Sihana."

"Check and mate!" Fanta declared.

Garrick hung up and made it a few more steps to *Pilgrim's Tale* when his phone rang again. It was his consultant asking if he could come in by the end of the day. It was already three o'clock, so getting to Tunbridge Wells would be a stretch, but he promised he would.

He stepped into the bookshop, the bell tinkling and, yet again, failing to summon John.

"John? It's David." He headed for the armchairs at the till. There was a partially opened box of books and another two new shade-less table lamps, made from reclaimed metal and sculpted into sinuous curves. To Garrick's eye, they looked like junk.

"Hello!"

Garrick jumped at the sudden voice from behind. John emerged from the back door, drying his hands.

"On tenterhooks today, are we?"

"It's been a hectic few days."

John indicated an armchair. "Then take a load off and let me put the kettle on. I have a new blend that arrived today."

"It will have to be another time. I have a consultant's appointment in Tunbridge Wells I must get to." He hadn't meant to touch his head, but did so subconsciously. John frowned.

"Ah. Perhaps later? My door's always open if you need to..."

"I appreciate it. I was going to ask you if you remember seeing this man," he showed him Mircea, "at the café with Stan?"

John nodded. "A couple of times."

"Great. Oh, and since I'm here, those books you've been reading on Romani culture. Can I borrow them?" Manfri and Duke's involvement was now at the heart of the case, so he thought it wise to research as much as possible.

John's face darkened at the implied sacrilege. "No!"

"Sorry, I meant *buy* them." Christ, John really was tight.

"Of course!" he brightened and looked around the room. "I have three of them, which I've finished with. Where are they...?"

Garrick glanced at the time on his phone. "I tell you what, I'll come back tonight and pick them up. And you can let me try that tea."

"Deal!"

Garrick caught the title of one of the newly arrived books in the cardboard box. "The life of Doctor John Stockton

Hough?" He picked it out. It was very old, and the cover was smooth and delicate. John quickly plucked it from his hand.

"Careful! That's quite valuable." He laid it carefully on the chair. "As are those books I'm selling to you. Hough's a fascinating chap. I shall have to tell you about him one evening."

Garrick stepped back, knocking one of the new table lamps over.

"Sorry. My coordination's shot lately."

"Watch what you're doing! I've been restoring them. I don't want to break them now that I have interested buyers."

"I'll get out of your hair then. Best of luck if you found suckers to buy these."

John pointed to the door. "Out, you philistine!"

27

I t was dark outside the third-floor window. Fresh snow was falling. It glittered when caught in the streetlights. Across the green, a steady stream of rush hour traffic moved up and down the slope of London Road. Everything in that frame, in that moment of time, was normal and uncomplicated.

"I wouldn't jump to any conclusions at this stage, David."

Garrick tore his gaze away and looked at Dr Rajasekar. His consultant was middle-aged, slender, with an angular face that enhanced her projected wisdom.

"Jumping to conclusions is part of my job," he said with a smile that didn't reach his eyes. His hands were clasped in his lap. His thumbs nervously circling one another. He was 41, but never had he felt more like a vulnerable child than now.

"Not in my world," Rajasekar snapped back. She gestured to her computer screen where Garrick's MRI result was rendered in three-dimensions. A small area had been shaded near the front. "The mass has not increased since the CAT scan, but now we have a better sense of its shape. This is your frontal lobe."

She used the mouse to spin the scan around. "The growth could be applying pressure, which would cause the headaches you describe, although I would have thought they'd be more constant. Perhaps the stress of work is a contributing factor. We shall get to the bottom of that," she added with a smile. "Any trauma to this part of your brain can lead to amnesia or psychosis. How is your memory?"

"I remembered to come here tonight." The doctor didn't seem to appreciate his joke.

"We have yet to locate the sarcasm centre of the brain." She peered over her glasses at him. "You could be the medical breakthrough we have all been waiting for."

A dose of gallows-humour is what Garrick needed. He felt his shoulders dip as he relaxed slightly. Dr Rajasekar gave a small smile of satisfaction when she noticed.

"And the psychosis?" Garrick prompted.

"Hallucinations, voices. The usual thing. Any sign of those?"

Garrick opened his mouth for a pithy comeback, but stopped himself. He shook his head. Despite the circum-stances, he was relieved he wasn't ticking off any of the symptoms.

"It goes without saying that you must contact me the moment you even think that is happening. There are other indicators to keep an eye out for. Delusions, paranoia, personality changes..."

"No. Unfortunately for my team, it's the same old me."

Rajasekar continued on without interruption. "Social difficulties, a lack of awareness or insights that you previously had no issues with, disorganised thinking..."

Shit.

Garrick shifted in his seat, his cheeks flushed, as if the temperature in the room had substantially increased.

"Are you alright, David? Would you like a glass of water?"

He shook his head. "I've been having a problem with the case I'm on. It's a complicated snarl of..." He stopped himself from giving anything away. "It's a murder investigation."

"I imagine that is the most stressful type of case to be on."

"It's never easy. But this one... I don't know if it's tangled up because of the case, or because of me. I keep having the nagging thought that I've been overlooking the obvious, or..."

"And has anybody else commented on this? Your superiors, for example?"

The morning's major detonation of the case aside, he had thought things had gone, if not well, at least in line with the normal meandering path such things tended to.

"No."

"Then I would put it down to stress. Complications of what you do, the few months you have had off from work and, of course, your sister. That is a lot, and I mean a *lot*, for anybody to process."

"What is the next step?" he tapped his skull, and this time swore he heard the tumour rattle. He hoped that wasn't the start of the hallucinations.

"We have to assess whether it is benign or malignant. Which means a biopsy."

Garrick tried not to entertain the thought of the doctors drilling into his skull.

"That's about all at this stage. I'll make arrangements as soon as possible. In the meantime, I'll prescribe something stronger for the headaches. Co-codamol should help. And keep taking the dexamethasone."

"Is that it? What else can I do?"

"I could tell you not to worry about it, but I think that would be pointless, wouldn't it? Other than that, I strenuously recommend you avoid head trauma of any kind. That includes impact sports. Even heading a football. If anything changes, let me know immediately."

Garrick thanked the doctor, and she walked him through the empty reception of her practice, where the receptionist had already turned the lights low before she had left.

"Good luck with the case, David. Perhaps one day you can look back on all of this and write a book about it."

He shook her hand and chuckled. "Weren't you the one on the search for the sarcasm gland? Maybe that will be your bestseller. You could be the next Doctor John Stockton Hough!"

She looked at him with a mixture of confusion and repulsion.

"What a peculiar thing to say."

Garrick shrugged, not entirely sure what he had said to offend her.

Dr Rajasekar's eyes narrowed. "You do not know who John Stockton Hough is, do you?"

In the cold air outside his consultant's private practise, DCI David Garrick stopped and watched his warm breath rise into the night sky. It was a sign he was still alive. For that, he must be thankful.

And now...

Now it was apparent how most people took life for granted. It was only when a life was taken, or the threat of it removed, did anyone stop and re-evaluate what they had. That was often when it was too late to change course.

He walked up the hill to his car and called DS Okon.

"We're keeping Stan Fielding in overnight for questioning and should have the paperwork through tomorrow so we can search the farm," she had told him. "Everybody is back on their feet here, sir. There's a feeling that this is it. Forensic evidence on the wounds is matching nicely. The only thing we don't have, are Fielding's fingerprints on the knife. If we had that, it would be case closed, lock him away, and throw away the key."

This was the first time he had heard Chib sound so jocular, and it suited her. He had no wish to pop her bubble, so listened with the occasional "*uh-huh*" or "*mmm?*" as she neatly parcelled the evidence away.

"What time will you be back here, sir?"

"I'm not sure, Chib. I have to pick something up."

He hung up when he reached his car. The snow was heavy now and he would be stuck in rush hour traffic too, so getting back to Wye would take a good ninety minutes if he was lucky. Plenty of time to think. Stuck in a traffic jam at Goudhurst, he called Chib's mobile and got her answer phone. He left a brief message.

A few minutes later, Fanta called him about their *special project*.

He leaned back in his seat, staring at the red brake lights of the vehicle in front, and listened.

It was almost eight o'clock when he parked outside the bookstore. As usual, the lights inside were on despite the late hour, enticing anybody inside who sought shelter. The snow had become a blizzard, and the white street had become almost indistinguishable from the snow-covered pavement. No traffic had dared disturb the veil. At the end of the street he could see the café, bathed in darkness. Wye was such a lovely small village, yet it had been the meeting point for people with such evil intent. People who took life for granted.

The doorbell gave its familiar tinkle as he entered. The heat and dim lighting from the assortment of lamps instantly made him feel drowsy. Hopefully, it wasn't a side effect caused by the lump in his head.

"John? It's me. Have you got those books?"

There was no answer. He strained to listen.

"John?"

He peeked into the backroom. The toilet door was ajar, and there was no sign of him in the cramped space he called a kitchen.

Garrick backtracked to the door and peered outside. The only set of tracks was his own, so nobody had been in or out for the last few hours. He walked down each aisle, stepping over piles of stacked book catalogued to John's own unique system. The lamps cast more shadows than the light they provided. He ran his hand over the soft velvet lampshade and considered pulling it off so it could offer more illumination.

"David?"

John Howard stepped through a door at the rear of the store, accompanied by a flurry of snow. He had changed out of his usual smart suit and into jogging bottoms and a white T-shirt. "I was out the back. I didn't hear you." He indicated the box Garrick had seen earlier. "I have those books for you. And..." He produced a sheet of paper and magically wafted it through the air. "An invoice for eighty-six pounds. I warned you they were not cheap volumes." There was a twinkle in his eye as Garrick took the paper. "You look like a man with the world on his shoulders. Sit. Let me make tea."

Garrick sat in the chair and toyed with the invoice, repeatedly folding and unfolding it. Neither man said much as John boiled the kettle, then poured it into his vertical teapot. He stirred it, then closed the lid.

"So what ails you?"

Garrick had known John Howard for years. John had even met his sister once when she had visited Kent to provoke another argument. They had never exchanged birthday or Christmas cards, yet there was an openness they shared.

"I have a tumour in my head," he finally said. "They don't know if it's malignant or not, but it's pressing on my frontal lobe. That means I could start to hallucinate, become paranoid, go crazy…"

John smiled and placed the teapot over a mug, and dispensed the brew from the bottom. He never offered milk or sugar. That would be a sin. He handed Garrick the mug and made one for himself.

"It sounds as if you are going to be more like the rest of us."

"Wouldn't that be awful." Garrick sipped the tea. It was sweet and had a slight nutty hint. John watched his reaction like a hawk.

"Good?"

Garrick sipped again. "Different," he said diplomatically as he fought the torpid atmosphere in the room. He was used to seeing John in a suit, but in a T-shirt, he could really see the old war vet had taken care of himself. His muscular arms almost filled the sleeves.

"Have you told anybody else about this?" John enquired.

"Until the doctor knows for sure what it is and how it's affecting me, there's nothing really I can tell people."

John closed his eyes as he drank his tea. "Mmm. Nice." He tapped the pile of books. "I was wondering why the sudden interest in the gypsies. Any progress in your case?"

"Plenty. All three girls were–"

"Three girls?"

"There was another this morning." John gently shook his head. "All asylum seekers. One had taken up with the Romani, and she was in a hell of a mess. The trucker who inadvertently brought her over was forcing her to sell drugs through the Traveller community. She wanted out; he didn't want her to leave."

"So he killed her?"

"That's how it seems. It appears one of the Romani elders wanted to take over the drugs run. One thing led to another, and the truck driver ended up killing him, while the girl ran. She was dead hours later."

"Terrible."

"Same cause of death as another poor girl before Christmas. She was working on a farm, which so-happened to have connections to the same truck driver. A Romanian. I showed you his picture earlier."

"I remember. I have seen him in the cafe. He was always fawning over that young girl who works there."

Garrick nodded. "That's the girl who was murdered this morning."

"I hope you have arrested him."

"And his co-conspirators."

"Bravo."

"Only, things didn't quite add up. We found the murder weapon, but it was impossible for the killer to have used it on all four victims, and the people we suspected were in custody."

"That is a problem. I can see why you're stressed."

"It was a speed bump. Or should I say, sleeping policeman. Me. I should have seen the connection. We arrested Stan Fielding."

"Stan? Now there's a turn-up for the books. He was more than your average racist, I grant you, but a killer..."

"I suppose once you kill, it's easy to kill again. Right? In the Falklands, how many did you kill?"

"They were vermin."

"They were people."

John shook his head. "They weren't British. The Argies were the invading force." He nodded to the boxed books. "You'll see how savage some cultures can be. I told you the Romani have heathen beliefs. Shaktism, animal sacrifice–"

"Like the *februa* Valentine's massacre you told me about in Rome."

"Exactly my point."

Garrick gazed thoughtfully at the lamp. "So you found buyers for all of this junk?"

"Yes. Shame. I was getting very fond of them."

"Your Mary Lynch collection." He wagged a finger at John. "I finally got it." When John didn't react, Garrick put his tea down and leaned forward in his chair. "Anthropodermic bibliopegy. Now there's a mouthful. I hadn't even heard about books covered in human skin." He noticed John Stockton Hough's book on the table next to John's seat. "And I probably wouldn't have if I hadn't seen that. A cover made from human skin. That's quite sick, if you think about it. What am I saying, it's very sick, full stop."

"It was accepted practice in the medical world. It's a tough coating. No different from leather if you think about it."

"And his first book was wrapped in the skin of Mary Lynch."

"She died of tuberculosis. And the skin was only from her

thighs, which Hough had preserved out of scientific curiosity."

"And later he bound three medical journals in her skin, just like any normal person would. And then there were the Nazis." Fanta had uncovered a complete menagerie of horror and recounted it with ghoulish glee. "Buchenwald concentration camp was said to make lampshades from the skin of butchered Jews. Ed Gein, murdered people in America, and used their skin to do the same."

John Howard didn't move. He didn't blink. He just gazed at Garrick with reptilian curiosity. Garrick picked up the lamp next to him and turned it back and forth, deliberately shining the light coming from the top of the shade into John's eyes, forcing him to squint.

"I had a look on eBay and couldn't find anything like them. Luckily, I have somebody back at the station who is a dab hand at navigating the dark web. It's amazing what you can find there."

John remained silent.

"Cat got your skin?" said Garrick with a snarl. "What sort of sick mind skins young girls for this?" He held up the lamp.

"Our country is overwhelmed, David. You and your type just ignore it. Gypsies, immigrants, all ruining our way of life. They should stay where they are. We can go to them. They don't have to taint our streets. And after we voted to be a United Kingdom once again, they still came over. Like vermin. Fielding and the others talked the talk, but they were too weak to do anything about it. Too greedy. They were earning a fortune off the backs of these detritus." Disgust dripped with every syllable.

"So you set them up."

"Somebody needed to take the blame. I facilitated. And it

would get rid of them and perhaps help keep our streets clean of the drugs and filth they were peddling. And with such a selection of beautiful colours parading through..." He smiled and pointed to the lamp Garrick was holding. "I think dear Galina casts a more vibrant hue across this room than she ever did in life."

Garrick shot to his feet.

John was quicker. He lunged forward, tackling Garrick around the waist. Both men slammed in a free-standing bookcase. It toppled over, cascading books onto Garrick's head. He dropped the lamp and tried to shield himself from further impact.

The bookcase collided with another behind, which toppled into another – spilling books in a grand domino run. The seven large bookcases fell, spilling their contents and smashing the lamps that had been decorating them.

Blood flowed down Garrick's scalp from where he'd been struck by the corner of a heavy volume. He felt groggy. Then powerful hands clamped around his throat. John was straddling him, choking the life from him.

He was too powerful for Garrick to dislodge. The calculated frenzy on his face was so focused on Garrick that he hadn't noticed flames from the pile of fallen books, ignited by the exposed bulb of a broken lamp.

They took hold of the dry pages in an instant. Thick black smoke curled towards the ceiling and enveloped a smoke alarm that had long run out of battery power.

Garrick felt the life crushing from him. His hand was touching something cool, the base of the lamp he had been holding. The shade was knocked free, exposing the lit bulb.

With a grunt, Garrick jammed the bulb as hard as he could into the side of John Howard's face. The man screamed as the glass shattered in his eye, the red-hot filament burning skin before it sparked with a loud pop as it electrocuted him. The building's circuit breakers snapped, preventing further power from flowing. With a squeal, John fell off Garrick and collapsed.

Garrick kicked the books off him and rolled onto his knees. The shop was full of smoke, forming a black barrier that slowly descended towards him as the fire rapidly spread. Orange flames consuming everything in their path and providing the only illumination now that the electrics had been tripped.

Breathing was impossible. Smoke was filling his lungs. He crawled to the door and tried to open it, but a fallen bookcase blocked it. Garrick was trapped.

With streaming eyes, he could barely see. He blindly groped over the books cast across the floor and found something big and heavy. An old tome about the Canterbury Trail. He hefted it at the window. Glass shattered and a snowy eddy gust into the room. He threw another book to clear a wider space and crawled over the broken glass to escape.

The snow was stained crimson from the cuts on his hands. He made it into the road before hearing feet running towards him.

"Sir?" It was Chib's voice. He had told her to meet him here, but she had been stuck in a jam on the M20. "David?"

She was nothing more than a blurred outline, backlit by a warm orange wall of fire that crept up to the first floor of John Howard's house, consuming everything in its path.

28

David Garrick hated hospitals at the best of times, and his private ward at William Harvey Hospital came top of the list. Overnight he had been on oxygen and his glass cuts stitched and glued together, along with a scar on his scalp from where a heavy book had struck him. All evening he had been in and out of consciousness.

It was late morning when he had felt well enough to sit up in bed so that DC Harry Lord could take his statement about what had happened. Harry sidestepped Garrick's own questions about the case. It became clear why just before lunch, when Superintendent Margery Drury came to see him. She had wanted to update him on the investigation herself.

"I didn't know if you liked chocolates," she said, taking the seat next to his bed.

"Love them."

Drury shrugged. "Oh well. I didn't bring any, so maybe next time."

She listened without interruption as Garrick talked her

through events from the moment he'd arrived at Sihana's crime scene. He edited the details of his appointment with Dr Rajasekar and highlighted the key information Fanta had churned up on the dark web. He was annoyed at himself for listening to John Howard's sustained disinformation about the Romani, all designed from the very beginning to subtly twist his thinking away from who the real culprits were.

Drury gave a little shrug and told him not to worry about it. They had all chased the bait. That morning Chib had led the search on Sam Feilding's farm. He was exporting wine, just as he said, but the vans that were returning back to the UK had been carrying drugs. The wine was a handy pretext to keep the supply route open. As far as they could tell, none of the workers on the farm had known about the contraband.

The Audi had been valeted many times by the poor, misused, cheap labour he was employing, but forensics had found traces of Duke's blood, presumably from the knife that had killed him. One of the farm labourers recalls John Howard visiting several times, and at some point the knife must've been passed back and forth between the men, but only Fielding could answer that one.

As for John Howard, he died in his shop as it burned down around him. The damage had extended to the building next door before the fire brigade had arrived to tackle the flames. There wasn't much left of John Howard, his lamps, or his books.

Garrick thumped his head back against the pillow. From all the head trauma he had sustained in the last few hours, it would be just his luck a pillow was the final nail in his coffin.

"So we lost all the evidence against him?"

"Not everything," Drury said with a playful smile. "There was a shed in the back yard that hadn't been damaged. He used it to store packaging boxes, bubble wrap, all he needed for online trade. It was also where he hung and dried the skin he cut from the girls. Sihana's was still hanging up. The lab boys are saying it's a treasure trove of DNA evidence."

She pulled a Mars bar from her pocket and slowly unwrapped it.

"I thought you said you didn't bring any chocolate?"

"Not for you." She bit into it thoughtfully. "This is what passes for lunch these days. I hate to say it, David, but all things considered, good job."

It didn't feel like it, but he didn't see the point in correcting her.

He was discharged by four o'clock and Drury had told him in no uncertain terms not to come back to the incident room for a couple of days. Chib was doing a competent job at winding down the investigation, and HR would roast her alive if she let him come back so soon.

He considered joining the team for Harry Lord's yet-again delayed birthday drinks, but he just couldn't summon the enthusiasm. He stopped off at the pharmacy to pick up his prescription of co-codamol and took some immediately. His head had been constantly throbbing since he'd woke that morning, but he hadn't had the courage to tell the hospital doctors.

He just wanted to go home.

That evening, David Garrick sat alone and in silence at his kitchen table. He'd intended to finish cleaning the fossil, but the shrill whine of the air pump provoked his headache. He must have stared into nothingness for a good half hour. Thoughts of the young girls who had been butchered on a whim came unprovoked. Young lives, all cut short.

He'd been forwarded an email from Fanta that she'd

obtained from the Royal Marines. It was a psychological report on John Howard after the Falklands War. He hadn't been the medalled hero, as he had always claimed. He'd been dishonourably discharged after being accused of executing young Argentinian prisoners. Nothing was ever officially proven, which Garrick thought was code for a military cover-up.

Another email outlined what the team was piecing together. John Howard had met Galina at Fielding's farm and charmed her to her death. That was his first attempt at removing skin. Jamal fell into his sights when he became embroiled with the gypsies passing through the village. Her connection with the Romanian was a bonus. Mr Constantine, as his business associates called him, represented everything John Howard hated. So setting him up to take the fall for the murders he was planning was surely a public service. The killing of Duke was a complication, but either way, it helped ensure the spotlight wouldn't be cast in his direction.

Desperate for some absolution, Mircea had started to talk in rather excellent English. He admitted to killing Duke, claiming it was self-defence. He had run after Jamal, chasing her down Castle Hill and into the retail park. Not to kill her, of course, but to convince her to stay with him. Only then had he become aware that John Howard had been watching everything from afar. From the moment they had met on Castle Hill, he had followed her into Folkestone. Mircea had watched Howard prey on Jamal and had fled before she'd been killed.

The answer to whether Sihana's death had been timed to mock Garrick's investigation, or if John simply couldn't resist, was something that had died with him.

Garrick closed the email. He didn't want to know any

more right now. He felt betrayed by a man he had known and trusted for years. A man he looked up to as an inspiration.

It was during this fugue he suddenly remembered the text from Wendy.

Are you doing anything this weekend?

He hadn't even replied. He hesitated, then typed: *nothing much. Fancy a better dinner?*

He pressed send before he could change his mind. Less than thirty seconds later, a reply:

Yes! x

Despite feeling like an emotional punchbag, David Garrick smiled.

Then his landline rang. He didn't know anybody who had the number – except the Americans. He hurried into the living room and scooped up the wireless handset.

"Hello, yes?"

There was silence on the other end. Probably an automated junk call trying to connect him to a pre-recorded message. He was about to hang-up, when he heard the distinct sound of movement on the other side, and a sharp distorted expulsion of breath across the microphone.

"Hello?"

A clunk, as if the handset had dropped, followed by more shuffling.

"Hello?"

Then, a voice:

"Davey..."

It was on the edge of hearing, so far away that it was a pale whisper. Then the line went dead. Had he imagined it?

With shaking fingers he dialled 1471, the British Telecom automated voice told him the time of the call but concluded, "we do not have the caller's number."

That's what it always said on international calls. Such as the ones from the American PD. Except this was very different. The voice he had heard... or *thought* he had heard...

It sounded like Emilie, but it was too faint to be sure.

But she had been the only person in the world to call him 'Davey.'

ALSO BY M.G. COLE

info@mgcole.com

or say hello on Twitter: @mgcolebooks

MURDER IS SKIN DEEP

DCI Garrick 2

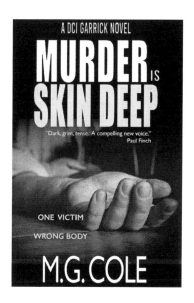

THE DEAD WILL TALK

DCI Garrick 3

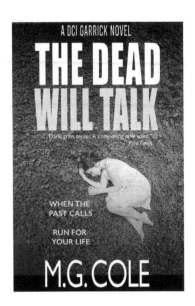

DEAD MAN'S GAME

DCI Garrick 4

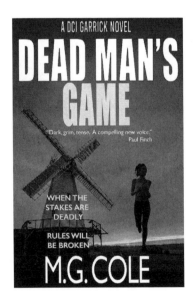

CLEANSING FIRES

DCI Garrick 5

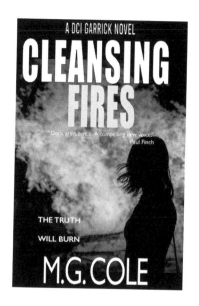

THE DEAD DON'T PAY

DCI Garrick 6 - COMING SOON!

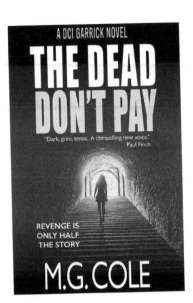

A DCI GARRICK NOVEL

THE DEAD
DON'T PAY

"Dark, grim, tense. A compelling new voice."
Paul Finch

REVENGE IS
ONLY HALF
THE STORY

M.G. COLE

Printed in Great Britain
by Amazon